# The Reason

Book One of the Just Say Yes Series

## Jen Andrews

# Dedication

*To my husband Jake, for putting up with me going crazy about this book series for months on end. For cooking me dinner when I wouldn't to do it myself because I didn't want to stop writing or editing. For ignoring me when I asked you to and for your never-ending support. I love you!*

*To Julie Brammer, you have been with me on this journey from the very beginning and I cannot thank you enough for your support. You have probably read this book more times than I have. Thank you for the late night calls and the lunch dates to go over changes. Your encouragement kept me going more times than I could ever say.*

# Acknowledgements

Thank you so much to my wonderful Beta Babes: Jessica, Emma, Karen, Casey, Judene, Melissa, MaRanda, Andrea, Veronica, and Chelle.

Big thanks to my friends who read The Reason and gave me the support and encouragement that I so desperately needed when I felt like my story wasn't good enough: Heather, Tiah, Shannon, Charity, Tiffany, and Cheri.

Thank you to these amazing ladies:

Kendra Gaither, at Kendra's Proofreading, Line Editing, and Reviewing- Thank you for beta reading and being a wonderful editor and friend! Thank you for all your advice, suggestions, patience, and for always being there to lend a hand, an ear, and a voice of reason.

Joann I Martin Sowles- Thank you for the endless questions you have answered, the comic relief texts, capes, boots, trucks and shovels, and for just being awesome!

Lindy Zart- You are one of my favorite authors, and I still cannot believe you read my book! Thank you for taking a chance and giving me great advice. I appreciate it more than you'll ever know.

Sarah Underwood- My Kiwi sister! Thank you for making sure that Andy's Kiwi/New Zealander side came through loud and clear. I cannot wait until we retire and live on the beach in En Zed, drinking wine, and lounging around while sexy Kiwi men read books to us. Oh, and we're definitely going to watch the All Blacks play some rugby!

Thank you to all the bloggers who have supported me, and the promotion of The Reason. I appreciate you so much!

Thank you to Sarah at Sprinkles On Top Studios for my beautiful cover. I could not be more pleased with how perfect it is.

Thank you to Tami at Integrity Formatting for making the inside of my books as gorgeous as the outside. You are a true joy to work with!

Last, but certainly not least. Thank you to all the musicians and bands that have inspired me and kept me writing. Thank you to Snow Patrol especially, for making great music and writing the best lyrics. You are the reason I started writing, and even though you will probably never see this, I will thank you anyway!

# Prologue

My eyes fluttered closed involuntarily, and I was in the dark again.

I heard sirens, and when my eyes would cooperate and open for me, I saw flashing red lights and my best friends crying while talking on their cell phones.

*This is bad.* I wanted to scream, to know what happened. *Why am I in so much pain?* My head felt like it was going to explode, my ribs hurt when I breathed, and my hip was killing me. I tasted blood in my mouth, so I ran my tongue over my teeth, praying they were all still where they were supposed to be.

*Oh God, why does my head hurt so badly?*

The black enveloped me again.

# Chapter One

Mommy hadn't been home for two days. I didn't know what day it was, I just knew that I was supposed to be in school, but wasn't. I missed music class and the hot, school lunches. I only had one friend at school, and I missed her, too. She was my teacher, Mrs. Cooper.

Before Christmas break, Mrs. Cooper bought me a new coat. It was pink and had white fur trim on the edge of the hood. Pink was my favorite color. I liked Mrs. Cooper and wished that she was my mommy. She was nice and she smelled pretty. She smelled like flowers.

My belly growled loudly, so I went to the kitchen to find something to eat. I was tired of potpies, so I opened the door of the fridge to see if there was any food. On the bare wire shelves, I found a jug of milk, a squeeze bottle of mustard, and leftover cake from my birthday.

A month ago was my eighth birthday, and our neighbor, Mrs. Francis, baked me a round birthday cake. It was chocolate cake with chocolate frosting, and she put a big candle shaped like the number eight on it. I had never eaten cake before, and I was sad that I didn't get to eat all of it.

Unsure, I poked at the cake with my finger. It was hard, and not soft and squishy like it had been when Mrs. Francis brought it to me, but I really wanted a piece, and I was hungry. The frosting was hard, too, and had greenish-gray icky looking stuff on it. It looked fuzzy.

After I had cleared a space on the messy countertop, I took the cake and milk out of the fridge and set them down. I pulled the drawer open to get a spoon to eat my cake with, but there weren't any in the drawer. We ran out of spoons a lot because Mommy used them for her medicine. She was sick all the time.

I took a fork and a knife from the drawer and set them down next to the cake and milk. Being eight, I wasn't tall enough to reach the plates in the cupboard, so I pushed a chair from the table over to stand on. The chair made a loud scraping noise on the floor, and it gave me goose bumps. Once I climbed up on the chair, I pulled a plate and a plastic cup from the cupboard and set them down on the countertop.

As I started to step off the chair, my right foot wouldn't move. I looked down in time to see that I was standing on the ear of my right bunny slipper with my left foot. Since I was already in the middle of stepping down, I fell off the chair and landed flat on my tummy on the dirty floor. My face smacked the linoleum hard, and I felt like crying, but I didn't because I didn't want to cause a fuss.

Even though I was home alone, I knew better than to cry. When I raised my head, I felt something dripping from my nose down to my chin. I wiped at my nose, and when I saw my hand, it had blood on it. I got scared and didn't know what to do, so I pinched my nose and went next door to see if Mrs. Francis could help me.

When I got to her door, my bunny slippers were wet from the rain and my feet were frozen. I opened the screen door and knocked quietly on the wooden door. I didn't want to make Mrs. Francis mad at me for being loud. She didn't come to the door. I turned to leave and when I let go *of the screen door, it slammed loudly. I ran down the sidewalk before I got in trouble.*

*"Zoey, honey, is that you?" Mrs. Francis called out to me. I was scared that I made her mad by slamming her screen door. Slowly, I turned back toward her, still holding my nose. Her face turned white, and her eyes got big.*

*Oh no, she's really mad at me! Letting go of my nose, I turned and ran to my special hiding place at home as fast as I could. Since my bed was just a mattress on the floor, I hid in my closet.*

*From my hiding spot, I heard knocking on the front door. She was calling my name. Her voice sounded funny, like she was mad, so I stayed quiet. As I hid, I watched the crack between the bottom of the door and the orange carpet of my floor. When a shadow passed by my closet door, I started crying.*

*"Zoey, sweetie, please come out so I can help you," Mrs. Francis said from inside my bedroom.*

She's not mad and she wants to help me?

*"Please, Zoey," she said, "I need to see if you're okay. Did you hurt yourself?"*

*My nose hurt badly and so did my chin. I wanted to let her help me, but I was scared and didn't want to get in trouble.*

*"Mrs. Francis, I fell off the chair," I said quietly from behind the closet door. "I'm okay. You can go home."*

*Again, I watched the crack under the door, until the shadow came back and stopped outside of my hiding spot. Nothing happened for a few moments, but then the doorknob turned, and Mrs. Francis slowly pulled the door open. She looked down at me sitting on my closet floor and made a sad face.*

But then something strange happened. She began to cry. Mrs. Francis quickly wiped her face and held her hand down to me.

"Let's get you cleaned up, sweet girl," she said quietly. Her voice was sad as she helped me up from the floor. "Where's your bathroom, Zoey?"

Not letting go of her hand, I led her to the bathroom. She picked me up and put me on the bathroom counter then found a washcloth and wet it with water from the tap. As she wiped the drying blood from my face, I heard the front door open.

A moment later, my mommy's laugh echoed down the hallway along with the laugh of one of her visitors. She always had visitors. They went straight into her bedroom and slammed the door shut. Everything was quiet as Mrs. Francis continued to clean my face, but then the gross noises started.

The man was making funny sounds and telling Mommy she was a whore, but I didn't know what that was. When she started making noises too, I hopped down and shut the bathroom door. She always told me to close the door when a man was there because she didn't want them to see me.

She made me be extra quiet, and I didn't want her to know Mrs. Francis was there, so I put my pointy finger up to my lips, "Shh," I whispered, so she knew to be quiet too. She nodded and continued to clean off my face. Just as she finished, the bathroom door flew open, and it scared us so bad we jumped.

"Who the fuck are you?" the gross man asked from the doorway. He came inside the bathroom, and he was naked. I slapped my hand over my eyes and gasped.

Mrs. Francis grabbed me, picked me up, and quickly took me out of the house. I uncovered my eyes when the cold air from outside hit me and made me shiver. She carried me to her house, and once we were inside, she set me down and locked the door behind us. She took my hand, led me to the kitchen, and asked me to sit at the table while she went to speak to Mr. Francis.

While I waited, Mr. and Mrs. Francis talked in the living room. They were trying to be quiet, but I still heard them.

"Michael, that child can't weigh more than forty-five pounds! She's eight years old, for crying out loud! Her mother is strung out on something, and we just had to hide in the bathroom while she had sex with some disgusting man!" Mrs. Francis said loudly.

"Calm down, honey, she'll hear you. Call the police instead of CPS. Tell them she's being severely neglected and not fed," Mr. Francis said. "They'll have to do something this time."

While Mr. and Mrs. Francis talked, I looked around the kitchen. It was clean, and not like the kitchen at my house. My house was dirty, and there were bags of smelly trash piled in the corner. At this house, in the corner was a small table with a pretty plant sitting on it. I wanted a closer look and tiptoed over to the plant. The plant had pretty, white flowers with purple in the middle.

"Zoey, are you hungry?" Mr. Francis asked from the kitchen door.

I nodded, and he went to the fridge, pulled a dish out, and put it in the microwave. While the food cooked, he came to stand beside me.

"It's called an orchid," he said and pointed to the plant. He told me they were Mrs. Francis's favorite flowers, and he'd bought it for her birthday.

"It's real pretty," I said as the microwave chimed.

Mr. Francis went to the microwave, pulled the dish out, and set it on the table. He poured two glasses of milk and sat down.

"Zoey, our lunch is ready," he said.

It smelled good, and my belly growled again, so I hurried to the table and sat down with him.

"Is Mrs. Francis having lunch, too?" I asked.

He shook his head as he scooped some macaroni and cheese from the dish onto two plates. He placed one in front of me and the other in front of himself. "She's making some calls right now. Maybe she'll join us in a bit." He smiled as he tucked his napkin into the top of his shirt and picked up his fork. "Dig in, sweetie," he said. "My wife's mac and cheese is the best."

Just like Mr. Francis had done with his, I tucked my napkin into the top of my jammies and started eating. I had never tasted macaroni and cheese the way Mrs. Francis cooked hers. The noodles were different. Not like the kind I ate at home. It tasted good, so I ate faster. I ate until my belly hurt because it was the best thing I had ever eaten.

"Zoey, do you want to watch a movie on TV with me while my wife finishes with her calls?" Mr. Francis asked when he finished his lunch. There was no TV at my house, so I was happy to watch with him. He let me pick out a movie from a big cabinet in their living room.

When the nice lady in the fancy suit came and knocked on the door, I had been sitting on the couch in my jammies and bunny slippers, singing. I was memorizing the song "Somewhere Over the Rainbow" because I had just seen The Wizard of Oz for the very first time.

The pretty song was stuck in my head because I wished that I could be just like Dorothy, and a twister would pick me up and take me far, far away from my house. The lady in the movie with the green face and the tall, black hat scared me though. She reminded me of my mommy when she got mad and yelled at me.

The lady in the suit came to talk to me and asked me a bunch of questions about my mommy, her visitors, and school. I answered all her questions and told her the truth.

When she was done talking to me, she made a call in the kitchen and then came back to me.

"Zoey," she said in a quiet voice. "I'm going to take you to a place that's called a foster home. Do you know what that is?"

I shook my head, and she went on to tell me that Mommy wasn't taking care of me the way she should, and that I would go live with another family while they tried to help her get better. "Does that sound okay to you, Zoey?" she asked.

"Yes," I said quietly. It was hard not to cry, but I didn't want her to be sick anymore, and I wanted to go back to school. Once the nice lady let me say goodbye to Mr. and Mrs. Francis, she took my hand and led me outside to her car.

While sitting in the car, I looked over at my house. There was a policeman there, and he was taking Mommy and the man that came into the bathroom to his car. They both had their hands behind their backs. Another man in a suit came out with them and got into the front seat of the car where I was. A police car was parked in front of us and my mommy saw me as she waited to get inside the police car.

"Zoey! What have you done to me, you little shit?" she yelled, and it caused me to jump. "Zoey! You fucking little brat! This is all your fault!" She continued yelling my name until the policeman pushed her head down and shut her inside the back of his car.

She yelled bad words and screamed at me from the back of the police car. I could see her jumping around and kicking the windows to get out.

"Zoey!"

"Zoey!"

"Zoey!"

# Chapter Two

## November 2011

"Zoey."

Something smacked me on the face as I slowly woke from my dream about my birth mom.

"Zoey."

*Whack!* Another smack to the face, this time whatever it was hit my forehead.

"Zoey!"

Someone laughed, and then a man's voice said, "Knock it off, Adam!"

*Smack!* Something hit my chest.

"Zoey!"

A warm hand gripped my shoulder and shook me. "Z, wake up."

After I rubbed my eyes and opened them, I stretched my arms over my head as I continued to wake up. My brother, Jeremy, was knelt on the floor at my side, shaking me.

"You fell asleep on the couch in the lounge. You okay?"

"Yeah, what time is it?" I asked and glanced around the customer lounge at the shop. The last thing I remembered was sitting down to flip through a magazine until closing time.

"It's almost five," Jeremy said. "Mom's here and she wants you to go somewhere with her."

When I sat up, I noticed that the couch and floor around me was littered with balls of wadded up paper. I picked one up and looked questioningly at my brother.

He shrugged and smirked. "Adam was trying to wake you up."

I heard a chuckle, and glanced over at the entry door of the lounge. My younger brother, Adam, was there with a big, stupid grin on his face.

"What's wrong, Adam?" I asked sarcastically. "You scared to get junk punched again?"

Jeremy laughed. "Dang, Z! That was so fuckin' funny when you did that."

The last time Adam woke me up, he scared the hell out of me, and my instant reaction was to start swinging. He got punched right in the crotch. It was his own fault, of course, and I didn't feel bad about it.

"It was not funny at all!" Adam growled from the safety of the doorway. "I'd like to have kids someday!"

"Oh fuck, *please* do not breed," Jeremy said to Adam. "We don't need any more of you in the world. One is more than enough."

Adam flipped us off and left. Jeremy and I laughed until our mom came into the office.

"Mija, come on. Let's go shopping," she said and tossed my purse onto the couch next to me. Jeremy pulled me off the couch, slung my purse over my arm, and gave me a shove toward my mom who was already leaving the lounge.

"Have fun, you two," he called to us as I wondered where the fuck I was being dragged off to by my mom.

Twenty minutes later, I stood next to my mom in the paint section at a home improvement store, eyeing her curiously.

"Why are we doing this again?"

"Because, Zoey, Andy will be starting his job at the shop next Monday. He won't have time to do any of this on his own, and you know the apartment needs some color. His final day at his job was last Friday, and he's taking Thanksgiving week off to spend with his family. He'll be moving *here* this weekend."

My mom was referring to the new guy, Andy Tate. Andy was my dad's newest mechanic at our family business, James Racing, where my dad and four brothers built and worked on drag racing cars.

The realization of what day it was finally hit me. *Shit! It's already Monday of Thanksgiving week!* All I wanted to do was go home and crawl into bed. I was tired and depressed and didn't want to be away from home. There were too many people around, the store was too loud, and I needed to be alone.

Unfortunately, my mom had other plans for me. I only had a few days to whip the four-room apartment above the shop into shape and make it habitable again, all for someone we didn't even know. It had been empty since I moved out after my dad and I bought the building next door to the shop. There were two nice apartments on the second level of that building, so I moved into one and rented the other to two of my best friends.

Three-quarters of the bottom level of the building was a warehouse, and the front part of the building was a store. My dad and I owned and ran a side business of James Racing, Inc. that we named "The Speed Shop." We sold high performance auto parts for racing. It made sense to have the store there. My brothers would always have the auto parts they needed, and the do-it-yourself mechanics who built their own cars would have access to everything they needed, instead of having to order online. We sold oil, accessories, and general maintenance items for cars, too.

"Why is Dad taking such a special interest in this guy?" I questioned, dragging my mind back to what I was supposed to be doing.

"Because, Mija," she said. "He doesn't know anybody here. What family he does have lives in Sonoma, so he is coming here all alone."

My dad had been raving about Andy for the past several days. He was happy about getting a new mechanic because the last few hadn't worked out so well. One of the last few was my loser ex-husband, Rob. The other two were either lazy or just couldn't handle the job. Dad was very meticulous about hiring this time, and I hoped that Andy was going to be a good fit at the shop working with my four brothers.

My dad was trying his hardest to retire from the business, and no longer worked on the cars, but he filled in when he absolutely had to. During the drag-racing season, the shop was very demanding, so we really needed five full-time mechanics. My brother, Jason, was one of the top engine builders on the west coast. With Jeremy's help, they'd earned quite the reputation for building top of the line motors. Adam and Noah did all the electrical work and custom projects on the cars they built.

Mom recently decided to update the furniture in the shop's customer lounge, so she was giving Andy the nice chocolate brown leather couch, coffee table, and the two end tables that were in the lounge. Damn, I was gonna miss that couch. I wondered if she'd let me take that couch and give him mine instead. Nah, I wouldn't wish my couch on anyone. I hated it. It was fine to sit on, but you'd need a chiropractor and a deep tissue massage to recover if you accidentally fell asleep on it. Which, unfortunately, I did at least once a week.

Funny thing about my depression, I fell asleep at odd times, and then couldn't sleep when I needed to. To put it bluntly, it fucking sucked.

*Stay focused, Zoey.*

The inside walls of the apartment were already painted a neutral, creamy beige color, so Mom and I decided to paint accent walls in the living room and bedroom. We also decided to paint the entire kitchen and bathroom to brighten up the small spaces. She'd given me a five hundred dollar budget to buy paint and other items to spruce up the apartment.

With my *mad skills*, as my best friend, Jess, liked to say, I had no doubt I would be able to get everything within my budget, and the apartment would look great. Decorating had become a hobby of mine over the years, and I was always helping family or friends pick out paint schemes and décor for their homes. It used to be fun for me, and it kept me busy from time to time.

Then everything turned to shit again, and I rarely went anywhere. I went to work, and then I went home. It was apparent that my mom was just trying to get me out of my apartment by having me do this decorating project.

Mentally, I was in a major funk. It all started eight months ago when my ex, Rob, decided to try to take everything that I'd worked so hard for. Luckily, the issue was taken care of after a couple months, but it was still a painful memory and caused me to have some trust issues again.

Slowly, I started sinking to a place I hadn't been in years. I felt alone, but I did it to myself. I didn't want to cause any more issues for my parents after everything they'd done for me. They were my saviors, and I owed them my life. Being depressed, I didn't feel like spending time with my friends anymore either. I just wanted to stay home and be alone. I had my apartment, my iPod, and my guitar.

I was okay with that for a while, but knew I needed to attempt living my life again. It was hard to make that step after being depressed for so long. *Maybe I should get a cat.* Suddenly, I pictured myself as a crazy old cat lady. *Yep, scratch that. No cat.*

"Zoey, what do you think of these?" my mom asked as she dragged me in front of a giant paint sample display.

"They're nice colors, Mom. I think I can work with them," I said to appease her. *Let's get this over with so I can go home.*

We chose four different colors for the apartment and took their sample cards to the customer service counter to get the paint mixed. The couple in front of us in the line was bickering about which shade of white paint they wanted for their home. Stifling a giggle, I glanced over at my mom who was grinning and rolling her eyes.

My mom, Luisa Rodriguez-James, was born in Mexico, and the house and town she grew up in was extremely colorful. We had an inside joke about how boring white walls were because my parents didn't have a white wall in their house. Well, except for the ceilings, of course, but who looked at those anyway? *That's right. I do...every fucking night.*

Once we finally turned in our paint sample cards, we were told it would take around an hour to get them mixed, so we went to a home-furnishing store to buy the rest of the items on my mom's shopping list. We found several of the items on clearance, so we were actually able to buy more than we'd anticipated. Andy would be getting a nice bedding set and several towels in addition to all the furniture my mom gave him.

Since Adam had recently moved in with his girlfriend, Angie, my mom was giving his entire bedroom set to Andy as well. Even though we didn't know him, I hoped that Andy would like everything in the apartment. We finished our shopping and went back to the home improvement store to pick up the paint.

"I really love this teal color you chose for the bedroom, Zoey," my mom said happily while we loaded the paint into my dad's truck. "It reminds me of the ocean down in Cabo. You are going to love it, too, when you take your vacation in a couple of months."

My depression had made my parents convince me to take some time off. I would be leaving at the end of January to stay with my Aunt Maria and Uncle Victor at their home near Cabo San Lucas, Mexico. How I let them convince me to stay there for an entire *month*, I would never know, but I was going to do it and hoped that it would get me out of the mental funk I was in.

"I'm excited to see it for the first time, Mom," I said, hoping I convinced her that I really was happy to be taking a vacation.

On the way back to the apartment, we swung through the Dutch Bros. drive-thru and spent the last ten dollars from our shopping excursion on two Cocomo coffees. I hadn't slept well the night before, so I was a bit sleepy and needed caffeine. Plus, being woken up so rudely from my nap at the shop by Adam hadn't helped.

# Chapter Three

When I pulled through the back gates at the shop, I honked the horn a few times to get my brothers to come out and help unload everything. They had a big job they needed to finish up on, so they were working late. Adam had already gone home, so Jason, Jeremy, and Noah packed all the heavy items up the stairs to the apartment. The apartment had no washer or dryer, so I decided to take the bedding and the towels next door to my place to wash.

As I juggled the enormous bags full of towels, bedding, and my purse, my dad called out to me, "Hey, Zoey, put some of that down and let me help you with it," he ordered me in his most loving, fatherly tone. "Your mom said you outdid yourself again with the paint and everything else you found."

I stopped at the edge of the small, grassy courtyard between my apartment building and the parking lot to let my dad catch up to me. When he did, I smiled at my favorite man in the world as he took half of the bags from me. "It's gonna look really nice once we get it all together, I think," I replied, grateful for his help.

"Glad to see you out and about, Zoey. We're happy you're willing to do this for Andy. You need to start getting out more, you know?"

He was right, and I knew it, but I wasn't sure if I was ready or not. "I know, Dad. Maybe this project will be the kick in the ass I need." I laughed but didn't want to tell him that I was doing the project for them and not Andy. It's not like I even knew the guy.

"That's my girl," he said with a genuine smile on his face. My dad and I had always been close and could talk about anything. I loved that about him.

When we arrived at the door of my apartment, my neighbor, Will, popped his head out of his apartment door when he heard us on the landing. "Hey, Zoey-girl! What-cha been up to? Ohhh, looks like you went shopping. What did ya buy?" he asked when he spotted the bags my dad and I both carried.

"Hey, Will," I said, happy to see him. "Mom and I bought some stuff for the new mechanic who's going to be moving into the apartment above the shop next weekend," I explained.

"Oh nice," he said. "Can't wait to meet our new neighbor and see what you've done with the place. Hopefully he's better looking than the last mechanic!"

"Well, I haven't seen him yet, so I honestly don't know." I chuckled and shook my head at Will's enthusiasm.

He and his boyfriend, Justin, were very dear friends of mine that I had met in high school when I joined the choir at my mom's insistence. They frequently got me off my ass and over to their place for dinner during the week. They lived right next door to me, so I couldn't avoid them the way I did everyone else.

After we said our goodbyes to Will, we dropped everything off in my laundry room and went back over to the apartment at the shop. By the time we made it inside, my mom had already instructed my brothers on where to put everything and had them assembling the new lamps we'd bought.

We discussed our plan of attack, and my mom forced my brothers into helping paint and move furniture since we had such a small amount of time to get everything finished. *Thank God they are helping.* I didn't have very much time to do it by myself, considering I worked full time, had my own business to run, and it was Thanksgiving week.

Once our plans for the apartment were made, I was getting ready to go home when my body rudely reminded me that I hadn't eaten since breakfast. My mom heard my stomach growl loudly and insisted that we all go out for pizza. I didn't want to go, but she left me no choice. Jeremy and Jason both got away with not going because Jason had to get home to his wife, Heather, and my two adorable nephews, Jake and Alex. I didn't want to think of where Jeremy was going when he said he had plans. I was sure he was off to visit his girl of the week.

Noah was engaged to my best friend, Jess, so he called her and invited her to come along with us. We took our seats at a long table at Rico's Pizza, our favorite pizzeria that just happened to be down the street from the shop. Once we'd ordered a couple of pizzas and a family sized salad to share, I decided to ask my dad about his new mechanic.

My curiosity got the better of me, damn it. It always fucking did, and I hated it. I had done all of Andy's pre-employment background checks and all that crap, but I paid little attention. I simply obtained the information we needed and put it in his file.

"He's originally from New Zealand, which was a surprise when I did his phone interview. He moved to the US about ten years ago, but still has a fairly strong accent. He was renting a room from his aunt and uncle in Sonoma. Luckily, he can work on both American cars and imports. It sounds like he just needed a change of scenery and found the job here from the online posting," my dad explained to me.

"Oh, and he's divorced, so he's single." He glanced over at me optimistically.

In response, I rolled my eyes and groaned. Everyone laughed, including me. If I did start dating again, I would definitely not be dating someone I worked with. "Well, I hope this one works out, Dad," I said honestly. "But, it's a pretty safe bet I will not have a relationship with anyone who works for you, ever again."

I thought back to the previous mechanics that didn't work out, and my mind drifted back to Rob. Young and dumb, I married the first guy who told me he loved me. What a waste of time that was. Rob and I met in high school, but waited for two years after graduation to get married. I attended college, crammed all my classes into two years, and got my degree in Business Administration. Rob went to the local tech school and started working for my dad at the shop.

One year into our marriage, I was miserable and considering divorce when I found out I was pregnant. Rob decided we married too young, and he was missing out on being young and partying with his friends. He didn't want to be stuck with a wife and kid at his age. He was out getting drunk with his buddies when I started cramping and bleeding. Jess took me to the ER, and I miscarried my baby at just over two months into my pregnancy.

All I ever wanted was to be a good mom. Better than the woman who gave birth to me and then failed miserably at raising me. I was devastated by the loss of my child, but I realized that everything happened for a reason and I shouldn't dwell on it.

Shortly afterward, I filed for divorce, but unfortunately, Rob didn't stay away.

Snapping myself back to reality, I sat and listened to my family talking and laughing. The server dropped off our food, and we enjoyed our family dinner out together. We stayed late catching up and talking about Jess and Noah's wedding the following June.

"Zoey, we need to hang out more," Jess whispered sadly. "I miss you."

"I miss you too, Jess. We should hang out soon. Maybe get Will, Justin, and Sasha together for dinner or something," I suggested. "We can do it at my place since the boys live right next door. They keep feeding me like I'm some sort of zoo animal," I joked.

Jess smiled at me. "That sounds fun, Z. Maybe we can break out the karaoke machine too!"

God, we hadn't done that in ages. "Sounds like a great plan, Jess." It really did sound like fun, and I missed my friends.

"Oh! You should do this dance class with me and Sasha!" Jess squealed. "It starts after Thanksgiving week and would be awesome to do together. It's on Tuesday and Thursday nights and lasts six weeks. You game?"

Not even caring what kind of dance class it was, the fact that it started next week was good enough for me. I knew I needed to get out of my apartment, so I asked Jess how to sign up for the class. She pulled out her phone and sent a text to someone. A few minutes later, her cell pinged with an incoming text.

She read it, and then turned to me. "Alright, Z, you're signed up."

That was easy.

Everyone had to work the next day, and I was exhausted, so I decided to call it a night and drove home in my 2011 Audi A4.

My sleeping habits were beyond my control, but I fell asleep within minutes every night. Staying asleep all night was the problem. I was restless and woke several times during the night for no apparent reason. Each time, I just laid there and stared at the wall, unable to fall back to sleep. At one point, I even tried pacing to make myself tired, but it didn't work, so I got back in bed.

Eventually, I fell back asleep, but then woke up yet again. This time, I stared at the ceiling. It was white and boring, and I considered buying some of those plastic, glow-in-the-dark stars and solar systems to stick up there, so I'd at least have something to look at.

As soon as my brothers moved all the furniture into the apartment after work the next night, I threw them out because they were annoying me and kept making fun of the music that I played on my iPod dock while we worked on the apartment. They had only painted one room, so it was up to me to finish painting and to clean the apartment before Andy arrived that weekend.

At least without them there, I could listen to my music and not be teased. They loved to tell me that I had 'Musical A.D.D.' because I listened to everything from classical music to death metal and everything in between, well, except for country music. I could not handle listening to songs about red Solo cups and sexy tractors. *Really? Sexy tractors? What the fuck?*

My obsession for the last few years was the band Snow Patrol. I was a sucker for creative and meaningful lyrics, and their songs were full of them. I was seriously addicted to their music and played it daily. Music was the only thing that kept me from going deeper into despair.

# Chapter Four

Waking with a start, and a very sore neck, on the couch late Saturday morning, I realized I forgot to wash all the towels and bedding we had bought for Andy's apartment. After spending Thanksgiving Day with my entire family, I went back to the shop's apartment and continued painting. By Friday night, I had the apartment painted and all the furniture arranged where I wanted it. I was dead tired from working full time and working on the apartment, so I had gone home and treated myself to a bottle of wine as I relaxed on my couch.

Of all the freaking places for me to fall asleep, and actually sleep through the entire night, it was on my damn couch!

Note to self: do not drink an entire bottle of wine when you need to get up early the next day.

"Shit, shit, shit," I grumbled aloud as I hurried down the hallway to the laundry room.

Andy was supposed to arrive later that night, and I wanted to get everything done in his apartment, so I would be gone before he arrived. I wanted to get back home and wallow in my own self-pity for the rest of the weekend. I really, *really* needed a vacation, or to get laid, as Jess and Sasha liked to tell me. *'Cause that worked out so well the last time.*

It had been several months since I'd even dated anyone, let alone had sex. I actually dated someone for a few months after Rob and I split, but it didn't work out. I don't even know why I bothered taking my birth control anymore. However, it did have other qualities I liked, and I just hadn't stopped taking it.

Maybe I needed a nice one-night stand. On second thought, that hadn't worked out so well for me either, and had happened clear back in high school...and landed me in therapy.

*Yep, I'm awesome. Not.*

Once I dumped the towels in the washer, I hopped into the shower under the hottest water I could stand to try to ease the kink in my neck from falling asleep on the couch. When I was finished with my shower, I dressed in some old jeans, a James Racing T-shirt, and my favorite pair of black low-top Converse shoes. My beloved Chucks. I kept, and still wore them, because they were my first-ever new pair of shoes and held great sentimental value to me.

By the time I choked down two brown sugar and cinnamon Pop-Tarts, the towels were ready to go into the dryer. It was already twelve-thirty, and I still needed to go check out the apartment to make sure everything was perfect. I transferred the towels to the dryer, and then tossed the sheets from the bedding set into the washer.

Luckily, I remembered to grab my iPod and my ear buds, so I at least had music to listen to instead of silence since I'd already brought my iPod dock home from the apartment. I packed all my cleaning supplies and strolled across the parking lot to the other apartment.

As soon as I walked through the door, I put my ear buds in my ears and cranked up one of my many playlists. I picked one with lots of upbeat music to keep me motivated, and then shoved my iPod into my back pocket.

Because I was a bit of a neat freak, I checked out the entire apartment to make sure it was spotless. It looked nice for the most part, but I decided to give the bathroom another good cleaning. Dirty bathrooms grossed me out, and I forgot to clean the bathtub and shower when I cleaned the first time. I sprayed the shower wall and tub with some cleaner to let it soak in for a while.

After I re-cleaned the rest of the bathroom, I went in and rechecked the kitchen. The kitchen was spotless, so I headed back to the bathroom and scrubbed the shower wall. Once the tub was finished, I was out of there. Fortunately, the kink in my neck had worked itself out from all the scrubbing I'd done, and I was in a good mood.

Getting down on my hands and knees, I started on the bathtub. "Bad Romance" by Lady Gaga came on, so I sang along out loud.

As I scrubbed the floor of the tub to the beat of the music, the bathroom light went off and immediately came back on. *What the fuck?* I froze mid-scrub and could *feel* someone behind me. My heartbeat quickened in my chest and the air suddenly felt thick. I was scared to turn around, but what choice did I have?

Slowly, I turned around to face the door, and there stood the most beautiful man I'd ever seen. He was leaning against the doorjamb with a huge grin on his face. His grin lasted about two seconds, and then a strange look washed over his face. His brows furrowed and he swallowed hard as he stared at me.

*What is that all about?*

As a wave of a panic came over me, I jerked the ear buds out of my ears. There was no way out of the bathroom, except past him.

Sure, he was sexy as hell, but I read that Ted Bundy was too, and he was a fucking serial killer! Plus, that weird change in his demeanor kind of freaked me out. He still stood in the doorway, staring at me with that same look on his face. It didn't appear that he was going to say anything, so I needed to do something.

"Who are you, and how'd you get in here?" I stammered, not knowing what else to say.

My heart thumped faster. I was positive that I had locked the door behind me when I came into the apartment. I realized then that he was holding a moving box. He blinked a few times, shook his head, and snapped out of his little trance. He smiled, and it somehow made me feel less threatened.

"I'm Andy," he said politely, with a *very* sexy accent. "And you are?"

He stared at me curiously again, and I wondered if there was something on my face, or if I'd sprouted horns since morning.

*Holy shit, he is sexy.* He had gorgeous golden skin, amazing blue eyes, and he wore his short, dark blond hair a little longer on the top. He was tall, too, at least six foot two or three. And the beard! *Oh my.* Well, it wasn't really a beard, but more like a sexy stubble that was just long enough to be soft.

When I stood, I took a quick peek in the mirror over the sink and walked toward him. There was nothing on my face and no horns on my head. *Thank God.*

"Hi, Andy, I'm Zoey James. My dad is Doug, the owner of James Racing."

*Duh, Zoey. He knows who your dad is. Chill the fuck out.*

Like an idiot, I held my hand out to shake his, not realizing I was still wearing hideous yellow rubber cleaning gloves. I quickly pulled my right glove off as he extended his hand out to me. It was warm and rough to the touch as he gently squeezed my hand.

"It's nice to meet you, Zoey. I'm sorry about turning the light off on you. I tried getting your attention, but you didn't hear me when I said hello. I didn't know how else to get your attention without scaring you."

Did I mention his accent was *very* sexy? I felt my face flush, and suddenly the bathroom seemed too small. *Why is he still holding on to my hand?*

"Sorry, I thought I'd be done in here and gone by the time you arrived," I said. He finally released my hand as I squeezed past him and into the hallway. "I'm almost finished." *Damn, he smells good.*

Everything felt weird with him in the apartment. I don't know *what* felt weird, exactly...but something was definitely going on. Maybe the fumes from the bathtub cleaner had gotten to me. I should have opened the window while I was in there. *Fuck, I'm probably high as a kite right now and don't even know it!*

Andy followed me to the living room and set his box down on the floor by the couch.

"I'm sorry. I guess I'm a little early. It didn't take me as long to pack my truck and trailer as I thought it would. I called your dad, and he told me he would let you know I would be here a few hours earlier."

I felt my back pockets and found only my iPod. I had left my cell phone at home. "Looks like I forgot my phone. Let me finish the tub, and I'll get out of your way."

He grinned again, his blue eyes literally freaking sparkling with amusement. *Crap, I can look at him all day long.*

"You're not in my way at all," he said with a slight smile easing over his face. "It's nice to have someone to talk to after being on the road alone for the day. Your dad says you live nearby, is that right?"

"I do. I live right across the way, in the brick building." I pointed in the direction of my apartment.

*Seriously? Can he be any sexier? Good Lord, Zoey, you act as if you've never seen a nice looking man before.* Okay, well I'd seen nice looking men before, but not one who looked like he stepped right off of a runway.

He was beautiful, sexy, and rugged. Masculine. *God-like.*

*Shut up now, Zoey. Jesus Christ, what is wrong with my brain all of a sudden? I've gone mad!*

His nose was a tiny bit crooked and had a noticeable scar across the bridge. It honestly made him sexier. *Oh, I forgot manly too.* He was wearing a black jacket, a dark gray T-shirt with some type of design on it, and perfectly fitted jeans, not too tight, and not too loose.

I continued my observation, and when my eyes found his feet, I noticed he wasn't wearing any shoes. "What happened to your shoes?"

He looked down at his feet and laughed. "They're by the front door. Kiwis don't normally wear shoes inside their homes."

Yeah, I had no idea what that meant. "Kiwis?" I asked, obviously thinking of the fruit. He chuckled. He probably knew I was thinking of fruit, too.

"New Zealanders refer to themselves as Kiwis," he clarified.

"I think I've actually heard that before, now that you mention it," I admitted.

*Good Christ, he is perfect. He's probably a dick, though.* Men that good looking always were. At least, in my experience they were. Although, he didn't seem like a dick, so I guess my rule contradicted itself.

*Yep, I've lost my damn mind, and I'm making no sense.* I needed to leave.

"I'll finish what I was doing while you bring in your boxes, and then I'll come give you a hand. I need to go to my place and get some things for you, too," I said, feeling my face flush.

He cracked a flawless smile again. "I can't believe how great the place looks, Zoey. Your dad told me it was a simple apartment with some hand-me-down furniture. I didn't realize it was going to be this nice. All the paint and furniture is great. I can't thank your family enough. I'm happy for the job, and the fact that there was an apartment to rent, too, made this a lot easier for me since I didn't have any time to look for a place to live."

His accent and deep voice literally rendered me speechless. I could sit and listen to him talk all day long. I needed to get the hell out of there, stat!

"Well, go get the tub finished," he said as I stood there, no doubt drooling while I listened to him speak.

"I'll pack in some more boxes." He moved toward me, and it broke my train of thought.

"Okay then, sounds good. And you're welcome...for everything." I smiled at him nervously, and then turned to go back to the bathroom.

Finishing with the tub in record time, I packed up all my cleaning supplies and was about to head out the door when Andy walked in. He had put his shoes back on, and I saw they were a worn pair of black Chucks. He was also carrying a guitar case.

"You play guitar?" I asked him, and he nodded. *Fuck me.* Why was it so hard to keep my damn mouth shut? "I play too," I blurted out stupidly. *Holy crap, Zoey. Shut. The. Hell. Up.*

He smiled at me in surprise and did this sexy eyebrow-raising thing. "Really? What kind of music do you play?"

*Run, Zoey. Run for the hills!* "I play acoustic, too, but not very well. I learn to play whatever songs I feel like singing," I admitted shyly. "I'm slightly obsessed with Snow Patrol right now, so I've learned to play a few of their songs."

*Shut the fuck up, Zoey!* I snapped my lips shut, hoping they would stay that way. I bit down on the insides of them, just to make sure. I would make them fucking bleed if I had to, as long as they stayed closed.

"You have?" Andy asked, and his gorgeous blue eyes sparkled with intrigue. "I like them too and can play some of their songs. I also have an electric guitar."

*Hmmm, what a nice coincidence. He likes Snow Patrol.*

"This is the last of my boxes," he noted. "I'm hungry. Will you go get something to eat with me?"

"Um, sure," I responded hesitantly. I didn't want to be rude to my new neighbor and coworker. "I need to head over to my place and change. Why don't you come with me, and we can get your towels and bedding from my laundry room."

*Deep shit, Zoey... Deep. Fucking. Shit. I've gone from running for the hills to having dinner with him, all within an hour.*

Fucking awesome.

# Chapter Five

Andy locked the door of his new apartment and walked with me to my place. We went upstairs, and he kicked off his shoes right inside the door. I secretly smiled about the habit of his. He followed me down the hall to the laundry room. The towels were dry, so I started to fold them.

"Let me do that so you can go change," he said. "It's the least I can do after all you've done for me."

I thanked him and hurried to my bathroom to clean myself up a bit. Once I ran a brush through my hair, I changed into a nice shirt and jeans. To finish off my outfit, I pulled on my favorite knee-high brown leather boots and brown leather jacket.

When I stepped back into the laundry room, Andy had already finished folding the towels and was putting his sheets in the dryer. "Did you pick this out, too, Zoey?" he asked, motioning to his stack of neatly folded towels.

I loved the way my name sounded with that accent of his. "Yes, I did. Do you like everything?"

"Yes, thank you. I can't believe you did all this for me. Everything you chose, I would have probably picked for myself if I'd done the shopping." He chuckled as he tossed in a dryer sheet and shut the dryer door. He even cleaned the lint trap before he pressed the start button.

"I'm starving, let's go eat!" He smiled as he gripped my shoulders, spun me around, and gave me a little shove out the door.

"I'll drive," I said with a laugh. He put his hands back on my shoulders and playfully propelled me down the hallway toward the front door. "Remind me never to stand in the way of you and food, okay?"

Andy let out a deep, hearty laugh. "Smart woman," he teased.

"An Audi, huh?" Andy asked as we arrived at my car. "I figured you'd be driving an old hot rod Chevy or something, since your family owns a drag racing business."

He didn't have any idea how close to home he'd hit with his comment. He opened my car door for me and waited until I sat down.

"I had one until about six months ago. Now, I only have my Audi. Let's go eat," I urged, trying to change the subject. "I don't want you to starve to death."

He closed my door, went around to the other side of the car, and dropped onto the passenger seat. He immediately pushed the seat all the way back because he was so tall. We talked for a few minutes about what to eat before we decided on going to my favorite steak house.

Nearing the door of the restaurant, Andy took a couple of long strides ahead of me and pulled the door open for me. *He has such good manners and is so polite.* As I walked through the door ahead of him, I caught the faint scent of his cologne again. It was a scent I loved and recognized from those scented cologne ads in the magazines we had in our customer lounge.

Plus, I was able to drool over Paul Walker's picture in the ads. I was a big fan of *The Fast and the Furious* movies.

Andy's warm hand rested on the small of my back as we entered the restaurant. Somehow, it made it under the back of my jacket, so there was only the thin layer of cotton from my shirt between us. My stomach fluttered at his light touch, and I felt my face flush again. *Holy crap!*

The hostess led us to a small table, handed us menus, and took our drink orders. "What's good to eat here?" Andy asked while looking over his menu.

"I normally get the house special steak with a salad and baked potato."

"Ah, a woman that eats and doesn't order only a salad. How refreshing," he stated. "I think I'll get that too."

The server came and took our orders, and then left us with more time to chat while we waited for our food.

"So, you're from New Zealand? What brought you to America?" I asked curiously.

"I moved here with my aunt and uncle when I was seventeen. They took me in after my parents and sister were killed in a car accident," he said, and a slight look of sadness fell over his face.

*Oh my God. That's horrible.*

The server arrived with our salads and a basket of bread. After she left, I gazed into his beautiful blue eyes. "I'm so sorry, Andy. I didn't know. Were you with them when it happened?"

"Yeah, we were in our car, and a truck came across the lane toward us at an angle. It hit the front driver side. They were killed instantly, but I was in the back seat on the passenger side, so I was the furthest away from the impact."

He motioned with his hands showing me how the cars had hit each other, so it was easy to understand what happened and how he survived the crash.

*Poor guy.* I felt the urge to scoot closer to him and hug him. But I didn't.

"I don't remember much of what happened, honestly. I was in the hospital for about a week after the accident. The medics were surprised to find me alive in the car after they arrived at the accident site, from what they told me. The glass from the windows cut my face, and I had minor internal injuries. My collarbone was my only broken bone."

He pinched his nose, right where the scar was, then ran his long, broad fingers across the stubble on his jawline. "I actually quit shaving to cover a couple scars," he disclosed as he glanced over at me. "They're faint now, but I'm so used to it I decided to keep it."

Unable to stop myself, I reached out and put my hand on his to comfort him. "Andy, I'm sorry. We don't have to talk about this anymore if you don't want to."

Not moving his hand, he smiled at me. "It's actually not so bad to talk about with you, for some reason," he admitted as he slowly rubbed his thumb over my fingers. He had nice manly hands. They were clean, and his nails were trimmed short. You would never know he worked on cars all day long.

"So, tell me about yourself, Zoey," he said, changing the subject.

Needing to break the physical connection with him, I sat back in my seat and pulled my hand away. I picked up my soda and took a drink, so it didn't look so obvious.

"Well, I was adopted by the James family when I was fourteen..." I started. He seemed intrigued, so I continued. "My biological mom was a meth-addict, and my father wasn't in the picture, so I spent six years in foster care before that."

After everything he had told me about the accident that killed his family, I felt a little uneasy talking about my life. Nothing that had happened in my life could have been anywhere near as bad as losing your whole family in the blink of an eye.

"Your dad mentioned you were married before. How long have you been divorced?" Andy asked hesitantly.

"Around two years," I answered, wondering why my dad would have told him that. I smirked inside when I remembered that my dad had told me Andy was also divorced. Was my dad up to something?

"Three and a half years for me," he said. "What happened, if you don't mind me asking?"

"I married someone who decided he didn't want to be married to me after we found out I was pregnant—"

"You have a child?" Andy asked, cutting me off. The surprise was evident on his face.

I shook my head and finished what I was saying. "Unfortunately, I had a miscarriage. After that, I filed for divorce and I've just been working at the shop and running my store since then," I expressed, frowning slightly on the outside, but cringing painfully on the inside.

"I'm so sorry, Zoey. That couldn't have been easy for you, especially on your own."

"Thanks. I've come to terms with it, but they say everything happens for a reason, I guess."

Andy nodded, "True, but no parent should ever have to lose their child."

He probably thought I was crazy. I was certainly wondering why in the hell I felt the need to blurt all of that out to someone I didn't know, especially after he'd told me his entire family was dead. I felt terrible for him because he had lost so much.

"No they shouldn't, Andy. But no child should ever have to lose his parents either." I could not imagine losing my family like he had his. The devastation would be too much to endure.

Neither of us said a word for what felt like an eternity, and I wasn't quite sure how to read the expression on his face since I didn't really know him.

"Well," he said after another minute, "we certainly are a pair, aren't we?"

Both of us let out a laugh, and it immediately eased the tension in the air.

"Do you have kids?"

"No, no kids," he answered. "We weren't married long enough to talk about having any." He seemed uncomfortable.

"How long were you married?"

"Six months," he said as our food arrived.

Once again, I'd skipped lunch, so I was famished. I quickly dissected my steak into bite-sized pieces and cut any tiny trace of fat from it. Andy watched me interestedly as I poured a little pool of A1 Steak Sauce onto my plate.

"I missed lunch again," I stated. He smirked and shook his head, and then started cutting up his own food.

"Would you like some dessert?" he questioned when he finished eating and was pushing his plate away.

"We can split something if you want, but you have to choose it." I wasn't picky about food at this particular restaurant. I was full, but something sweet did sound good.

When the server came back to take our plates, Andy ordered a slice of chocolate cake. Of course, it was my favorite. Chocolate cake with chocolate frosting. I chuckled to myself as I thought back to my dream the week before. *Who would've thought that a piece of moldy, chocolate cake would bring me to the place I'm at in my life? Guess that's just one more thing that happened for a reason...*

After dessert, the server dropped off our check at the edge of the table. I dug in my purse for my wallet, but Andy reached out and picked up the check before I could see how much my part of the bill was.

"Keep your money," he said, shaking his head. "Please, I'm buying."

I wanted to pay my part, so it didn't feel like a date, but I thanked him instead.

When we arrived back at my apartment, we went our separate ways in the parking lot. While I was fumbling with my keys at my downstairs lobby door, he jogged up to me.

"Hey, Zoey, what are your plans for tomorrow? I don't know where any stores are around here yet, and I need to do some shopping. If you don't have any plans, would you care to help me out, once again?"

"You happen to be in luck. I'm free all day tomorrow and have some Christmas shopping I need to do."

"Great, do you want to leave around nine?"

"Sure," I said and stepped through my now open lobby door.

"Goodnight, Zoey."

I smiled at him. "See you tomorrow at nine." I shut the door and leaned against it. *Oh, boy I am in trouble.*

When I made it upstairs and into my apartment, the intercom buzzed from the porch downstairs. I pushed the button and said hello.

"Hi, again. It's me." I instantly recognized his sexy accent. "I forgot to get my things from your laundry room," he said laughing.

"Oh yeah, you'll probably need those tonight. Come on up." I buzzed him in and left my door propped open. I walked down to the laundry room and checked the bedding in the dryer. The sheets were in a heap of wrinkles from sitting for too long, so I turned the dryer back on to try and get them out. I put the towels that Andy had folded in an extra laundry basket, so he could carry them home easily.

Right as I finished loading the towels in the basket, Andy stepped into the laundry room. "They're all wrinkled, so I turned them back on for a while. Want a beer while we wait?"

"Sure, that sounds good," he replied, and I brushed past him and back down the hall to the kitchen.

He leaned against the kitchen counter, while I dug two beers out of the fridge and opened them. I handed him one, and he followed me to the couch. I picked up my remote off the coffee table and pressed play to start my iPod.

We sat on the couch, drank our beers, and talked about music until the buzzer on the dryer went off.

"I'd better get home. I'm sure you want me out of your hair," he joked as we collected the basket from the laundry room.

*Um no, not really.*

"Again, I can't thank you enough for everything you and your family have done for me. I'll see you tomorrow at nine. Sweet dreams."

Then he was gone.

# Chapter Six

At seven the next morning, I woke to music blaring from my alarm clock. I had set it early, so I would definitely be ready when Andy picked me up at nine. I showered, dried, and then put on my favorite matching Victoria's Secret panties and bra. Not that anyone besides me was going to see them, of course, but they made me feel pretty and a little more confident.

After blow-drying my long, golden hair, I used my flat iron and straightened my natural waves. Lately, I hadn't been wearing much makeup, but decided to pay extra attention to my eyes. I curled my eyelashes just right and added an extra coat of mascara to make my big, baby blues stand out a bit. I even added a little bit of blush to my cheekbones for some color, since it was, after all, almost winter, and my nice California tan was fading. My trip to Cabo would take care of that.

I finished my makeup with some pink lip-gloss, and then went to my bedroom to pick out something to wear. I decided on a nice pair of jeans, my favorite brown boots again, a red, V-neck wrap around shirt, and my brown leather jacket. By the time I was ready, it was almost nine, so I went into the kitchen to wait for Andy.

Killing time, I checked my answering machine and found no new messages, but I did see several missed calls on my caller ID. I scrolled through the phone numbers, and every single call was from Rob. *Ugh, what in the hell does he want?*

Rob hadn't called me in months, which meant he was either calling to beg me to come back to him, or to be a total dick and completely insult me. Since he didn't get through to me, or leave a message, God only knew what he wanted this time. Since he'd already taken my prized possession from me six months ago, I figured he must want to try to win me back.

Great, just what I needed.

My intercom buzzed, so I picked up my purse and keys and skipped down the stairs to meet Andy.

"Good morning! How was your first night in the apartment?" I asked the moment I saw him. I was trying to be extra cheerful so he wouldn't see my irritation.

That irritation being Rob's calls.

"Wow, Zoey, you look amazing." He gave me a once over from head to toe with his gorgeous blue eyes. He shook his head as if he was trying to remember what I'd asked him. "Uh, I slept really well," he finally said. "Thank you. The apartment is very comfortable."

I seemed to have flustered him, so I gave myself a little victory cheer on the inside. *Ha! Take that, sexy man! You flustered me enough yesterday, so I think I owe you a few.*

"Good, I'm happy to hear it," I told him, deciding to play nice as we walked to the parking lot.

"After you," he said as he motioned with his left hand toward his awaiting truck. It was a nice, newer black Crew Cab Chevy.

"Nice truck," I said as he opened my door for me. "Is it the Duramax?" I asked, referring to the engine. Yep, with my dad and brothers all being mechanics, I was a little bit of a gearhead.

"Thanks," he replied with a smile. "It is a Duramax. I know it's a little big for living in the city, but I need it to tow my car trailer when I race."

My curiosity, again, got the better of me. "You drag race?"

He nodded. "I built a '69 Camaro a few years ago. I used to race it in Sonoma, and I'll probably start racing here in Sacramento, too. Will you come and watch?"

"Sure," I answered reluctantly. "I'm sure the whole family will want to watch, too. Let us know when you plan on going. You'll see my brothers out there, anyway. They're always helping out with the cars they build."

"So, what's on our agenda for the day?" I questioned. I stole a look over at him as we pulled out onto the street.

"I have nothing for the kitchen, so we should start there, I think," he replied. "I'll need pots, pans, silverware...everything. Oh, and food too, since I'm gonna need to eat."

"Priorities!" I joked as I thought back to our goofing around before we left for dinner the previous night.

"I'll need to go to a Target store or something, too."

"I think it can be arranged," I stated.

"Oh, good," he said as he scanned over a small strip of stores as we passed. "There's a Laundromat right there, not too far from home. That's good to know for laundry day."

"Hell no!" I shuddered at the thought of him stepping foot inside that place. "I went there a while back to see if they had the big washers to wash one of our car covers for the shop. That place is nasty. You don't want to go there. You can use my laundry room instead."

He frowned when he looked over at me. "Zoey, you've done way too much for me already."

"No arguing with me about this. Trust me." I laughed to help lighten up his mood. "If it makes you feel better, you can buy your own laundry soap and dryer sheets. *But* if you insist on going to the Laundromat, you might want to make sure all your shots are up to date."

He let go of the steering wheel, raised his hands in mock surrender, and grinned. "Okay, bossy. You don't leave me much choice."

"Can you turn in here, please?" I begged, pointing to the Dutch Bros. drive-thru. "I need caffeine. I didn't sleep well."

He flipped on his turn signal, turned in, and pulled forward to the drive-thru window. "What should I get?" he asked while looking over the menu board. "I've never been here before."

It was my favorite coffee place, so I pretty much ordered the same drink every time. "Do you like coconut and chocolate?" I asked as I dug through my purse for my wallet.

He smirked. "Yeah, who doesn't?"

I glanced over at him, and he had a big, sexy grin on his face. That's when I realized he was totally screwing with me. I shook my head and laughed. *Oh, he's a smartass, too. A sexy smartass though.*

Since I liked my coffee extra sweet, I unhooked my seatbelt and slid across the seat to place our order, which put me right next to him. *Dang, he smells good.* I stretched across his lap to get closer to the window and ordered two large Cocomo's with an extra shot of coconut in each.

While I was leaning across his lap, I felt his hand rest on my lower back. It sent chills up my spine and heat to other places I shouldn't mention. I didn't want to move back to my seat, but knew I couldn't stay sprawled across his lap, no matter how badly I wanted to.

At the window, the barista told me the total price for our coffees while blatantly ogling Andy. I handed her the money. Wow, I was the one who ordered and paid, and she never took her eyes off him. I was practically sitting on his lap, and I was completely invisible to her.

"You smell good," he whispered as we waited for the coffee.

"Um, thanks," I replied nervously. I was too close to him. *Holy crap, he thinks I smell good, and his hand is still on my back. Hurry up, coffee!*

When our order was ready, the barista handed us our coffees and my change. "Come back soon," she chimed as she batted her eyelashes and offered Andy her most flirtatious smile.

I giggled. "I think she likes you."

He shook his head and smiled before he took a sip of his coffee. "Thank you for the coffee, Zoey. I like it."

With my coffee in hand, I slid back to my seat. He laughed and pulled his truck back out onto the road.

Was this man completely oblivious to the effect he had on women? I sure as hell hoped he was oblivious to the effect he was having on me.

We headed to a kitchen store and proceeded to fill a shopping cart to near overflowing with pots, pans, dishes, silverware, and everything else he would need for a functioning kitchen.

"So, why'd your aunt and uncle pick Sonoma to move to?" I asked while we wandered around the store.

"My uncle took a job at a winery there, actually. We're originally from the Auckland area, and my dad and uncle ran one of the big vineyards there for years. After the accident, my aunt and uncle thought it would be better for me to start over somewhere new. They wanted to move where they could work in a winery. It's a family thing, and what better place than the California wine country, right?"

I nodded, understanding. "That's a long way to go for a job, though."

He winked at me. "Yeah, it was, but I think it worked out okay."

We decided to go to Target next, where I loaded a cart with toys for my nephews' Christmas presents. We filled yet another shopping cart of all the essentials for Andy's place, which included a new bottle of laundry soap and dryer sheets, at his insistence.

"Don't want you to think I forgot about these," he said and put them in his cart.

We pushed our carts in the direction of the checkout registers. I stopped at the end of an aisle because I saw a book I wanted to look at because Jess insisted it was a necessary read. I didn't know what it was about because I was out of the loop for newer books.

After reading the summary, I wanted to look at the second book of the series that was sitting on the shelf next to it. As I reached for it, I glanced down the aisle and noticed Rob standing in front of the magazines. He was flipping through a car magazine.

"Oh crap."

"What's wrong, Zoey?" Andy asked with a concerned look on his face.

"Over there, in front of the magazines." I nodded toward Rob. "That's Rob, my ex. He called me several times last night while we were at dinner, but never left a message. His number showed on my caller ID. I don't want him to see me."

"I think he's going to see you. He's coming this way."

"Shit!" I grumbled. I did not want a confrontation in public, especially in front of Andy.

Andy took the book from my hands, and then his arms wrapped around me from behind. He tilted his head down a bit and whispered in my ear, "Don't worry. I got this. Just follow my lead, alright?"

He slipped his warm hands inside my jacket across my stomach. I was too surprised at having his hands all over me to tell him no, so I nodded and went along with it. Plus, it felt nice, so...

Rob came around the corner of the aisle a split second later and found Andy draped around me.

Ignoring Rob, Andy kissed the top of my head, then pulled my hair back and nipped my earlobe with his teeth. *Oh hell, that was hot!* I swear on all that is holy, my knees trembled.

Freaking trembled!

"Zoey," Rob called out loudly. "Aww, look at you. Did you finally get over me? Sure took you long enough."

My mouth dropped slightly open in disgust as I glared at him. I was not going to take his shit in front of Andy and needed to stand up for myself.

"Really, Rob? Did you forget I was the one who filed for divorce? Not the other way around."

Rob shook his head and scoffed. "If that's what you want to think, babe," he retorted as he stepped closer to us. "I was long gone before that ever happened officially."

I wondered if he was trying to be intimidating by coming closer to us. It didn't seem to be working on Andy, if that's what Rob was trying to do.

"Hey, mate, you need to walk away," Andy stated calmly. He stepped beside me with his arm protectively around my shoulders. "Zoey has moved on with her life, so maybe you should too."

Rob backed away a step. "I already have, *mate*," he said, attempting to mock Andy, but it only made him sound like an even bigger ass. *What did I ever see in him?*

Andy dropped his arm off my shoulders and took a step toward Rob. Andy was easily five inches taller than Rob was, and outweighed him by at least forty pounds. *All muscle, no doubt.*

"She's all yours," Rob muttered. "Hope you like my sloppy seconds."

Aw shit, why did he have to say something so gross? Anger flickered in Andy's eyes as he took another step toward Rob.

I wedged myself in between them and faced Andy. "Please, he's not worth it, trust me," I begged, taking hold of his very muscular biceps. Andy didn't seem to hear me because he was too focused on Rob. Something in his eyes worried me a little bit. It was almost as if he wanted to rip Rob's head off and chuck it across the store.

I really needed to stop this before something bad happened. "Hey, Sexy!" I said suddenly and hoped it would get his attention. "Let's pay for this stuff and go home."

It must have worked, because a second later, he snapped out of it and smiled wickedly at me. "Now you're talking, Beautiful," he said, focused on me instead of the loser behind me. "Let's get out of here."

He gave Rob one last threatening glare, and we turned to leave. I pushed my cart ahead of me, and as we were walking away, Andy slung his arm over my shoulders and pulled his cart behind him with his other hand.

# Chapter Seven

Without another word to each other, we paid for our items and loaded everything into his truck. As soon as we were inside the cab with the doors shut, Andy turned to me. The expression on his face was so full of anger I couldn't make eye contact with him because I was so humiliated. "What in the hell was that all about, Zoey?"

"I am so sorry," I blubbered, trying to hold back tears.

God, I hated that man for turning me in to a crying idiot! It'd been months since I'd seen him, and with one little encounter, I was freaking out.

"One minute, he acts like he hates me, and then the next minute, he tells me he loves me and wants us to be together. I don't know why he does that. When I remind him of how things really happened with us, he gets belligerent and insulting."

One tear slid down my cheek, but before I could wipe it away myself, Andy brushed his thumb across my cheek to wipe it away for me. I felt the heat rise in my face from his touch.

"You just told me he's not worth it, Zoey. Take your own advice."

"I know, but I'm still so embarrassed. I barely know you, and here you are, almost getting in a fight with my stupid ex-husband." I started crying then.

He moved across the seat closer to me and pulled me in close to him. I slid my arms inside his jacket and wrapped them around his waist. I could feel his warmth and strength through his shirt. It had been too long since I had actually let someone comfort me. I couldn't help it, so I gave in and rested my cheek against his chest. His heart was still racing from the adrenaline pumping through him.

Andy made me feel safe and not quite so lonely. I was completely at ease with him, and it scared the hell out of me. This guy was off limits for so many reasons.

"Zoey, please don't be upset. You didn't do anything wrong. That guy is a fuckwit for treating you the way he did and needs to have his ass kicked for it." He took in a deep, calming breath and let it out. "Let's go get some lunch and try to unwind for a while. I've worked up an appetite, and you shouldn't be skipping lunch again because of me."

"Okay. That sounds nice." I didn't dare tell him I skipped breakfast. I let go of him and wiped my tears away with the backs of my hands.

He slid back to his seat and started his truck. Andy had shifted into reverse to back out of the space, when Rob pulled up behind the truck in my old, black Chevelle.

"What the fuck does he want now?" Andy growled when he realized it was Rob.

He stomped his foot down on the gas pedal, and I thought he was going to slam right in to the side of the car as the truck lurched backward.

"Please don't hit my car!" I cringed and covered my eyes, so I didn't have to witness it.

He hit the brakes, and I uncovered my eyes. "What do you mean *your* car?" he asked, confused, as Rob gunned the Chevelle and sped away.

"That's my car he's driving," I admitted. "Well, it's his car now, but my dad and brothers built it for me, and I don't want to see it get all smashed."

"Why does he have your car?" he asked, still confused.

*Oh God, I want so badly to tell him. I need to tell someone.* Only my family knew what happened, and that was only because they were involved.

I took a deep breath and slowly exhaled. "He has it because he sued me and my dad around eight months ago. It was the only way he would leave me alone."

Andy scowled at me in utter disbelief.

"He filed a lawsuit against us, saying it was partly his idea to open The Speed Shop," I clarified. "He said we owed him money from it, since we were still married when I opened the store. The only way he would drop the lawsuit was if I gave him my car as his payment. We contacted a lawyer, and legally, he could have taken half of the profits from when we were married, so it was easier to give him the car and be done with it."

When I looked up at Andy, I saw he was dumbfounded by my admission. "Andy, I willingly gave it to him. I opened the business with the help of my dad and could not risk it. He had so much more at stake than I did, especially since his name is attached to my business *and* his own business. I signed the car over to

Rob with no regrets. He signed a contract with the lawyers, saying I had paid him what I *owed* him. Legally, he cannot get another cent out of us. I have no regrets in my decision to give him the car."

"Was that what you were talking about last night when you told me you owned a hot rod until six months ago?" he asked dryly.

"Yes." I nodded as another tear rolled down my cheek. "Can we go, please? I'm done talking about this for now."

He gave up. "Alright, let's get some lunch. For the record, I wasn't going to hit your car. I was only trying to scare him, so he'd back off and leave you alone."

We headed toward home, and on the way, Andy pulled into the parking lot of a sandwich shop. We went inside to the counter to place our order. "I'll just have a Coke. I lost my appetite." I sighed and pulled a few dollars out of my purse to hand to him.

He refused my money, so I left him standing at the counter and found a table for us. Andy shook his head and ordered his sandwich.

After he got his food and filled our cups at the soda machine, he sat across from me at the table. I glanced at his tray and saw he had ordered the biggest sandwich I'd ever seen in my life. They cut it in to four pieces because it was so big.

He took one section of it and set it on the table in front of me on top of a few napkins. "Eat," he insisted, pointing to the sandwich in front of me.

"Yes, sir," I teased. "You're kind of bossy, you know?" I took a drink of my Coke, unwrapped the sandwich from the paper, and then took a giant, exaggerated bite to make him happy.

"So, Zoey," he said, smirking. "You think I'm sexy, huh?"

I almost choked on the bite I had taken and remembered I called him "sexy" at the store to divert his attention from Rob. I didn't know what to say to him, so I smiled and chewed my food...and blatantly ignored his question.

Thankfully, a minute later, my cell phone rang. Thinking it might be Rob, I checked to see who was calling first, but it wasn't. It was my friend, Ben, and I hadn't talked to him in months.

"Do you mind if I get this?"

"Nah, go ahead," he replied and continued to eat while I answered my cell.

"Hey, Ben, it's been a while." I noticed Andy's eyebrow rose when I said Ben's name. Dang that was sexy!

"Zoey, how are you doing?" Ben asked. He sounded somewhat desperate, like he needed something.

"Not too bad, you?" I answered back.

"I'm doing fine, but I have a bit of a crisis and I need you."

*Interesting...* "What's up?"

"Can I ask a huge favor from you? Please tell me you don't have plans next Saturday night."

Oh, you know me, *loads* of plans. "Nope," I stated bluntly. "I have no plans Saturday night. I'm free, what do you need me to do?"

Ben let out a long sigh. "Oh, thank you! The band has a gig for a twenty-fifth wedding anniversary party, and Jenna needed to go out of town for a family emergency. She doesn't know when she'll be back." He was referring to his back-up singer, Jenna. "It's an eighties themed party, and you are the only person I know who can handle it. You'd be saving my ass, and of course, I'll pay you."

I laughed because I would do it for free, just to get away from the confines of my too silent apartment. "Sounds like fun to me," I told him truthfully. "Can you text the song list to me, so I can make sure I know all of them?"

He sighed with relief. "I love you, Zoey! I'll send it to you today," he said. "Thank you."

I ended the call, happy and nervous.

"What was that all about?" Andy asked curiously.

He had the longest, thickest eyelashes I had ever seen on a man. *Focus, Zoey, the man asked you a question.*

"Looks like I get to sing at a party next weekend."

He almost seemed relieved. "I thought you were making a date with someone," he admitted.

Why would he care?

As we finished our lunch, I told him about the party. Ben sent me the song list, and I was good to go with the songs, as I already knew them all. He also let me know to wear a black dress to the party, so I would match what the rest of the band would be wearing.

I laughed as I visualized the entire band, and myself, wearing matching black dresses, with our hair slicked back like the all-woman band in the Robert Palmer music videos from the eighties. I knew Ben meant the men in the band were going to be wearing black clothing, not black dresses, but the way he worded it in the text really made it sound funny.

I drifted back from my daydream to find Andy picking up my iPhone from the table. "What are you doing?" I asked suspiciously.

"Putting my cell number in here," he replied. "You can ring me anytime if your ex starts giving you shit again."

It took him an awful long time to put his number in my phone. A devious look came over his face and he chuckled, then raised my iPhone up and snapped a picture of himself with it.

He was adorable and amusing, and I swore again that I could watch him all day long.

Satisfied with the picture he took, his fingers moved quickly over the screen, and *his* phone rang. He hit the end call button on my phone, set it back on the table, and then picked up his phone and punched in a few commands on it.

There I sat, grinning like an idiot, completely amused by him, trying to figure out what he was doing. With absolutely no warning, he held up his phone and snapped a picture of me before I could stop him.

"Hey, no fair!" I protested, with the stupid grin still on my face. "You didn't give me time to pose and try to look good. Let me see." I tried unsuccessfully to snatch his phone out of his hand.

"Don't worry, you're beautiful," he said with a laugh as he stared at his phone, his blue eyes shining with adoration.

*He's the beautiful one, not me.*

I picked up my phone to see what he did to it, but before I figured it out, he put his phone up to his ear. My phone rang as I held it in my hand. Well, it wasn't ringing exactly. It was playing the song "I'm Too Sexy" by Right Said Fred. The picture he snapped of himself also displayed on the screen.

"Oh my God! You're an ass!" I was laughing so hard, my eyes filled with tears and I snorted. Embarrassed, I dropped my phone back onto the table, covered my face with my hands, and continued laughing.

"Are you gonna answer, or leave me hanging, Beautiful?" he grinned devilishly.

Why did he keep calling me beautiful? Finally, I picked up my phone and hit the button to answer his call, even though he was sitting across the table from me.

"Hi, Sexy," I kidded.

He looked me straight in the eyes, and not putting down his phone, he said, "Thank you for finally answering my question."

I knew exactly the question he was referring to, and yes, I thought he was the sexiest man I had ever laid eyes on. I had from the second I saw him standing in the doorway of the bathroom in his apartment.

"You're welcome," I replied and quickly hit the button to end the call.

His mouth dropped open slightly in shock. "Did you really just hang up on me?" he asked. "That's messed up." Then he smiled and hung up his phone. "Let's finish our lunch and go shopping."

Who knew I would have so much excitement helping someone shop?

Next, we stopped at the grocery store, where I picked out my favorite vegetables and a few other groceries I needed. I noticed Andy was selecting many of the same items I did. We walked around the store, dropping things into his cart.

"So, Zoey, what's your favorite food?" he asked, trying to make small talk.

"Mac and cheese," I answered without even thinking about it. "In fact, I think I'm gonna make some for dinner. A big salad, too." Since we were on the pasta aisle, I grabbed a bag of noodles for the macaroni and cheese and tossed it into the cart. "We'll have to go back for some cheese," I said, since we already went through the dairy section.

"You're not going to make it from a box?" he asked.

"No. Homemade mac and cheese is the best. Plus, I really don't like food out of boxes." Well, except for Pop-Tarts, those were my weakness for food out of boxes. Yet, I felt the need to explain myself to him. "When you live your entire life, well, until the age of twelve or thirteen, where ninety-five percent of your food comes out of a box or a can, you get tired of it."

He seemed intrigued.

"My birth mom and the foster families I lived with weren't much into fresh fruits, veggies, and meats. I would much rather make everything homemade. Besides, it's healthier, too." I shrugged and dropped a block of cheese into the cart.

"Wow, I sound like a total snob, don't I?" I questioned when he didn't say anything right away.

"No, not at all," he replied uncomfortably. "It makes sense, actually. You're right, Zoey. That would suck, and I'm sorry you had to live like that for so long."

"It wasn't that bad, because I had food and people who took care of me better than my birth mom did. It could have been much worse," I admitted. I might have never been put into foster care, which would have left me stuck eating cheap potpies from the microwave and neglected for the rest of my childhood.

We finished our shopping at the grocery store and headed home. Stopping at my apartment first, we took my groceries upstairs and put them away. Next, we headed over to Andy's apartment and hauled an entire truckload of new items and groceries up to his place.

While Andy was putting away his groceries, I unpacked his dishes and silverware and filled the dishwasher for him. I planned on hand washing the pots and pans, since they wouldn't fit in the full dishwasher. While the sink was filling, I checked my phone and noticed I missed a call from Ben.

I shut off the water and called him back. "Hey, Ben, sorry I missed your call."

"Thanks for calling me back so quickly," he said. "I talked to the couple who's having the eighties themed party next weekend, and they've added a few songs to the list. Do you think you can sing the lead on them? Women originally sang them, and I would love it if you would be willing to sing them. What do you think?"

"Yeah, Ben, that sounds great, actually. Is everyone getting together to rehearse this week? I can come over, and we can run through all the songs."

"Great, Zoey, I really owe you for this. What nights are you available?"

Ha! More plans for the week. We made plans to rehearse on Wednesday and Friday nights, since I had dance class with Jess and Sasha on Tuesday and Thursday.

When I was washing the pans, Andy came to help me when he was finished with what he was doing. It felt weird to be standing side by side with him, yet, at the same time, it felt like it was a normal, everyday occurrence. When we were done, and the pots and pans were dried and put away, we collapsed on the couch, both exhausted from our day of shopping. He reached over and picked up something off the end table. He handed me a book.

It was the book I had in my hand when we saw Rob at Target. "What are you doing with that?" I asked.

"Don't you remember me taking it from you at the store?" He wore a sexy grin on his face again.

*Um, no, not really...* Right after we saw Rob, Andy's hands were all over me, and my earlobe was in his mouth. I would have been surprised if I could have remembered my name at that moment. I shook my head.

"I guess I threw it in my cart and bought it for you," he said.

"Um, thanks...I think. Sounds like it's going to be a really busy week for me now," I said nervously and stood to leave. "I should probably get home. I have a few chores I need to do before I can cook dinner."

"Thanks again for everything, Zoey," he said as he rose from the couch. He pulled me to him and hugged me. "I don't know what I would have done without all your help."

*He* was thanking *me*. All I helped him with was spending his money. He helped me with so much more.

"It was a good day. Well, except for the whole Rob scene," I said, suddenly feeling bad about it again.

Andy must have sensed it, because he gave my shoulder a comforting squeeze and brushed my hair behind my ear. "Hey, remember what you told me. He's not worth it. Don't give it another thought. Remember what I said, too, and call me if he gives you shit again."

After I went home, I threw a load of laundry into the washer, and then called my mom.

"Hola, Zoey," my mom exclaimed happily when she answered. *Gotta love caller ID.*

"Hi, Mom," I said. "I wanted to let you and Dad know that Andy's all moved in."

"Oh, I'm glad to hear it. Did you meet him yet?"

"Yes. I did. We spent the entire day together, shopping for things he needed for his apartment. He even took me to dinner last night." I went on to tell her about everything that happened with Rob but omitted the hot ear-nibbling part, of course.

"I'm glad he was with you, Zoey."

I was glad he'd been there too. "I'll see you at work sometime tomorrow, Mom. Have a good night. Love you."

"Goodnight, Mija," she replied cheerfully.

I mixed some fresh ranch dressing for my salad, and then started making the mac and cheese for dinner. I decided to throw two gigantic chicken breasts in the oven to bake, too. At least I would have leftovers for lunch tomorrow.

Wondering if Andy was going to fix dinner at his place or not, I sent him a text before I changed my mind.

*You cooking anything for dinner? Come over if you want. Dinner is at seven.*

# Chapter Eight

A few minutes before seven, my intercom buzzed. It was Andy. "Hey, I would never turn down a home-cooked meal. I brought drinks, too," he said. I hit the button and buzzed him into the building.

Even though I spent the whole day with him, I felt like I wanted to spend more time getting to know him. We were neighbors and coworkers now, after all. Yes, that was me making excuses to spend time with him. *Shit...*

After I let him in, he kicked off his shoes and joined me in the kitchen. He leaned against the counter and watched me work on dinner after I refused to let him help.

A few minutes later, there was a knock at my door. "What the heck?" I stated nervously. Nobody had access to the building without a key or being buzzed in by Will, Justin, or me. I looked through the peephole and was pleased to see my neighbors on the landing outside my door.

"Hey, guys, what's up?" I asked as I opened the door. "Come on in."

They came inside, and Justin was the first one to speak. "Hey, Zoey, we just wanted to check up on you. We saw a superhot guy walking across—"

He stopped talking when he caught sight of Andy standing in the kitchen. An excited expression washed over his face when he turned to face Will and me. "Well, I guess we know where the hot guy went, Will," he announced enthusiastically. "Zoey, are you gonna introduce us, or what?"

I silently hoped he wouldn't drool on my floor. "Guys, this is Andy, the new mechanic my dad hired. He's renting the apartment over the shop, too." I was trying to be nonchalant about it. They were constantly on my ass about getting out and dating, and I didn't want them to get their hopes up, especially since there was a hot man standing all sexy-like and looking completely at home in my kitchen.

They shook hands and introduced themselves to one another. I was unsure if Andy had heard Justin say he was superhot. He didn't let on if he had.

Will and Justin sat on the barstools at the counter, talking with Andy about New Zealand, while I was getting dinner ready. I laughed to myself as I heard them convince Andy to teach them a few slang words and sayings that were common in New Zealand. They seemed to be having a good time together, so I continued to prepare dinner.

Since I made a ton of mac and cheese, and it would take me days to eat it, I decided to see if the guys wanted to stay for dinner. "Do you two want to stay for dinner, since you're here?" I asked Will and Justin. It was the least I could do for them feeding me all the time. "There should be enough, if you don't mind splitting a piece of chicken with each other, and there's plenty of mac and cheese."

"You had us at mac and cheese, Zoey," Justin admitted. So easy to please that guy.

After the food was ready, we sat down and had a nice dinner together. We were all getting to know our new neighbor, although, it sort of felt like a double date, since Will and Justin were a couple.

Andy had brought over some beer and a bottle of Johnnie Walker, so with the food and drinks flowing, I was really enjoying myself. We told Andy all about our days in the high school choir together and even sang a few songs for him at his insistence.

Luckily, I had a buzz. Otherwise, I never would've had the nerve to sing in front of him.

After dinner, I went to the kitchen to load the dishes into the dishwasher and left the men to hang out. Justin came in to help me, leaving Andy and Will in the dining room, both of them laughing their asses off about something. Andy had a great laugh. It was deep and sexy.

"Zoey, it's so nice to see you looking so happy! Are you and Andy seeing each other?" he asked.

"We only met yesterday, Justin," I stated, surprised by his question. "Besides, he works for my dad, and you know what happened with Rob. I am *not* going down that road again."

Rob could've taken a lot more than my car. He could have taken my store, which was a business my dad co-owned. He could have ruined my dad's business, too, if things hadn't ended the way they did. I knew I would never put my family or myself in that position again.

In the process of what Rob did to me, he had knocked me down a peg or two, so I had a hard time trusting people.

Rob didn't deserve a cent, because he put no time, effort, or money into The Speed Shop. I did the majority of the work, with my dad helping with the startup costs and co-signing on my loan. My dad was a silent partner and only stepped in to help when I asked for it. We had a great working relationship, however, he could still get hurt financially, if my business took a hit.

It wasn't that I thought Andy was like Rob. They were nothing like each other.

*"Earth to Zoey..."* Justin said in a goofy singsong voice while snapping his fingers in front of my face. The thoughts about Andy and Rob disappeared from my head.

"Sorry!" I laughed, realizing I had completely tuned him out as I immersed myself in my thoughts. "Justin, I know where you're headed with this," I whispered to him, not wanting Will and Andy to hear me. "I do like Andy. He's a great guy. Do I think he would pull the same shit Rob did? Hell no! But, he works for my dad, and after what Rob did this morning, I have no intention of being involved with someone I work with." *Again.*

Justin raised his eyebrows, and I knew by the look on his face that he was going to get pissy. "What the hell did Rob do this morning, Zoey?"

I explained to him what happened at the store, and what Andy did to get Rob off my back.

"Face it, baby girl. That sexy beast in there just might have the hots for you, and you would be crazy not to act on it. If he did what you said he did, and he only knew you for twenty-four hours, I'd say you can trust him not to fuck you over."

He was right. I shrugged, not really wanting to continue the conversation because it was depressing. I knew I could never become romantically involved with Andy as long as he worked for my dad.

Justin got a nasty grin on his face. "You can at least give him a blowjob after what he did for you this morning."

I smacked him hard on the arm. "You are not right in the head, you know that?" My face got hot and it was, no doubt, bright red from embarrassment. "Besides, I've never given one before," I whispered. I really was buzzed, because every tiny thought that popped into my fucking head was coming out of my damn mouth.

Justin raised his eyebrows. "Well, the first thing you wanna do is..." He went on to explain to me how to give the perfect blowjob, in graphic detail.

I was too intrigued and laughing too hard to care how embarrassed I was by the conversation. I had been married before, but I wasn't experienced when it came to anything other than good old missionary position. Besides, Rob only cared about getting himself off, so I spent the majority of our marriage completely unsatisfied in the sex department.

From the dining room, Will bellowed, "Hey! What's taking you hoes so long in there?"

"Mind your own business!" I yelled back. "I'm learning how to give blowjobs in here!" Ouch, that sounded really, *really* bad. *Good going, Zoey. Must...stop...drinking...*

Suddenly there was a commotion coming from the dining room. Chairs scraped across the floor, and heavy footsteps thundered toward the kitchen. Andy and Will fought each other through the doorway between the dining room and kitchen. Andy won.

Justin and I laughed at them. "Jesus, you two," I squeaked. "I'm not learning how to give one *literally*! He's gay, remember?" I blurted out, pointing at Justin.

By the time I finished my sentence, we were all in hysterics. I swore I saw a relieved expression pass over Andy's face. I sent the men back to the dining room while I finished in the kitchen.

When the dishwasher was loaded, I rejoined them for a few more drinks. By the time we finished off the beer, and most of the bottle of Johnnie Walker, I was close to being drunk. Unfortunately, the alcohol was making me extremely tired. It had been a long week, then a long weekend, and we had to work the next day.

Andy noticed I was fading fast, because he spoke up, "We'd better get out of here, guys. It looks like we're losing her." He was completely adorable with a happy grin on his face and sleepy blue eyes from drinking.

They stood from the table and put their empty beer bottles in the recycle bin. I walked them to the door and held it open as they made their exits. Justin and Will both gave me a hug and wet sloppy kisses on the cheek.

Andy gave me a hug, too, but the kiss I received on the cheek from him was not wet and sloppy. He rested the palm of his big hand on my cheek, and his fingers tangled slightly in my hair. His warm lips brushed my cheek, and it made my skin tingle.

"Thank you again, for everything, Zoey. I don't know what I would have done without you this weekend. I'll see you tomorrow."

"Goodnight. Come see me in the office tomorrow morning. We'll do your paperwork and get your uniforms ordered." He nodded his head and started down the stairs.

"Hey, Andy?" He stopped on the stairs and looked back up at me. "Thanks again for this morning with Rob. I'm glad you were there."

He smiled at me and gave me a little wave. "Me too. Sleep well, Zoey." He continued down the stairs and out the lobby door.

After shutting and locking my door, I went to my room and got ready for bed. I was too tired to add anything to my daily journal, but I did decide to change the ringtone Andy had set for his calls on my cell. The one he set was funny, but definitely not fitting for him. It didn't take me long to find the perfect song for his ringtone, and I decided it would be my song of the day, too.

"Sex on Fire" by Kings of Leon.

# Chapter Nine

The next morning, I woke up feeling tired and a little crabby. Maybe it was a hangover. *Who knows?* Again, I did not sleep well and woke several times during the night. Each time, the first thought that entered my mind was about what Rob had done, and how sweet it was for Andy to defend me.

It took a while for me to get back to sleep each time, so I had plenty of time to think about how great Andy was. I knew I shouldn't think about him as anything other than a friend, though.

All the festivities of the previous week and weekend had finally caught up with me. My muscles were sore from cleaning, painting, and being tense, so I spent a little extra time in a hot shower after I dragged my ass out of bed.

Sitting down on the shower seat, I turned on the body jets installed in the wall and enjoyed a nice back massage to ease some of the fatigue. I finished my shower, dried off, and pulled on my cozy, hot pink, fleece robe from Victoria's Secret.

My days with my birth mom, then my days in foster care, made me appreciate the nicer things in life. Until my adoption, I never owned anything new. Shit, I never *owned* anything. My former foster parents let me *borrow* items that previously belonged to someone else. No matter what foster home I went to, I was always wearing someone else's old, unwanted, underwear, socks, and clothing.

Aside from my old black Chucks, I liked to treat myself to new, girly, pretty clothes. They made me feel good and gave me a bit of a confidence boost that I truly needed, even if it was something simple, like my favorite pajamas, which were simple tank tops and boxer short sets from Victoria's Secret.

I worked my ass off, so I deserved it, right?

Suddenly, I found myself wanting this funky depression to stop. I decided that as soon as Andy was squared away at work, I would call my hairdresser to see if I could get my hair cut and styled later in the day. With the anniversary party coming up, I needed to look presentable for it as well.

Stepping from my bathroom to my bedroom, I slipped my robe off and let it drop to the floor. I dressed in a matching bra and panty set, a pair of jeans, and a James Racing T-shirt for work. Once dressed, I returned to the bathroom and applied a bit of makeup, and then combed and blow-dried my hair straight.

My stomach growled loudly, begging for food, so I headed to the kitchen, turning on my iPod when I walked past the dock. With plenty of time before I had to be at work, I made a cheese and mushroom omelet and a bowl of fruit for breakfast.

Sitting alone in the dining room eating, my thoughts kept drifting to Andy. He was undeniably sweet, gorgeous, sexy, and virile. Truthfully, he seemed to be the perfect package.

He would definitely make a wonderful boyfriend for some lucky girl. It just wouldn't be me.

My cell phone pinged with a new message, breaking my train of thought. *Thoughts I had no business having.* I forgot where I left my cell the previous night, especially once we started drinking.

After searching for five minutes, I finally decided to call my cell from my home phone. I found it in the living room between the couch cushions. How it ended up there, I would never know. I touched the screen to find I had missed eight calls and two text messages.

I cringed when I scrolled through the missed calls. They were all from Rob, of course, and he didn't leave a message. Big surprise. I'd considered changing my number several times, but it was too much of a pain in the ass. Deleting Rob's messages was easier than having to send out my new phone number to everyone.

There was a text from my mom telling me she would be late to the office, and I would need to get started with Andy's paperwork and new employee spiel on my own. *No problem, I can handle that.*

It would be nice to spend a few minutes alone with him. I knew it was stupid of me to think it, but I couldn't help it. I knew we could never be anything more than friends, and I was getting a little bit ahead of myself. He might not even be attracted to me, but I was definitely attracted to him. *Crap. I need to get my mind straight.*

I thought back to the previous night, when he kissed my cheek. I knew he probably did it because Will and Justin both did as they were leaving...but, holy hell. My face flushed at the thought of his warm lips on my skin, a hint of Johnnie Walker still on his breath, the sexy as hell stubble on his face, and the way it tickled as it brushed my skin.

Did I mention the way he touched my face? I loved the way his palm rested easily against my cheek, with the tips of his fingers in my hair, and the way my entire body tingled when his fingertips grazed the same earlobe he gently bit.

*Holy fucking hell.* I was going to need a cold shower. *Or sex. Lots and lots of sex with the very nice looking new neighbor.*

My cell phone pinged again with a text, snapping me out of thoughts that were very quickly turning pornographic in my head. *Speaking of the sexy new neighbor...* The text was from Andy.

> *Good morning. Did you eat yet? Getting ready to fix something if you want to come by. Had fun last night with you and your friends.*

I messaged him back.

> *Sorry, just finished eating. Yes, it was fun last night and they are great aren't they? See ya in a bit. 8 am sharp!*

He sent a text back with a smiley face and a message.

> *:) Yes ma'am! Who's being bossy today?*

Guess it was my turn to be bossy for the day. He was bossy with me the previous day at lunch, when he made me eat part of his sandwich. I definitely won't forget to eat with him around, although that might not be a bad thing. I pulled my pants up from my lower hips and decided to go put on a belt. It seemed I had managed to lose a few pounds over the last several months.

I arrived at work around seven-thirty and decided to clean the office. Finding the spray cleaner and a towel, I dusted all of the surfaces of the desks, and then swept the floor. It didn't take long at all, and by the time I was done, it was a few minutes before eight, and my brothers were loudly making their way through the back door.

They must have met Andy outside and introduced themselves already. Noah held the door open, while Andy and Jeremy pushed a giant rolling toolbox through it.

"Thanks for the help," Andy told Jeremy and Noah as they showed him where to put his toolbox at the back wall of his new work bay.

The James Racing shop had five large work bays. There was one for each of my brothers, and then one for Andy. Each bay had a car lift, and the mechanics brought in their own toolboxes and tools.

At the opposite end of the shop, there was another large bay for the dyno machine, where they measured the torque and horsepower on the drag cars. The mechanics could make the necessary changes to the engines to get the cars running to their best performance potential by using the dyno machine.

Directly behind the bays was a large machine shop, where they custom built anything they needed for the drag cars. Next to the machine shop was our break room, newly refurbished customer lounge, and the office. The lounge had large windows facing the shop bays, so the customers could see the mechanics as they worked on their cars if they wanted to.

While my brothers helped Andy get situated in his new work area, I went out to the front of the shop to pick up the mail out of the locked mailbox. On the way, I stopped at the main entrance and asked our front desk girl, Mandy, how her weekend had gone. We talked until the phone rang, so I waved goodbye to her as she scheduled an appointment.

I hadn't picked up the mail in a few days, so the stack was huge. I went back to my desk and absentmindedly opened all of the envelopes. My mind wandered to everything that had happened over the weekend.

As I was sorting the mail into stacks of junk, bills, and magazines, I remembered I wanted to get my hair cut. I made a quick call to Autumn, my hairdresser. She had just had a cancellation, so she made an appointment for me at noon.

Standing up from my chair, I looked through the window to find my brothers still showing Andy around. They seemed to be getting along well. Not wanting to intrude on their 'man time,' I sat back down to pay some bills. Right as I finished, Andy came inside the office.

"Hey, Zoey, how's it going?" he asked, smiling down at me from where he was leaning in the doorway. "Sorry I'm late."

"No worries," I replied in regards to his tardiness. "I see you and my brothers became acquainted out there. That's great." I motioned for him to take a seat in the chair next to the desk, and he came in and sat down.

"I have your paperwork and some other information to go over with you, and then we'll get your uniforms ordered," I said, trying to be professional. What I really wanted to do was reach out and— well...I really wanted to strip his clothes off to see if the rest of his body was as insanely good looking as his face.

*Holy hell, Zoey!* I took a deep breath and got my shit together. I went over all of his paperwork with him and filled out his tax forms.

"We contract with a company for your uniforms, and they'll supply you with ten of them," I explained. I glanced up from the paperwork in front of me, and he was trying to hold back a smile. *Why in the hell is he looking at me that way?*

He noticed my discomfort and gave me a big grin, his blue eyes sparkling.

Flustered, I took another breath and shuffled the papers on the desk in front of me. "You'll be responsible for bringing the dirty uniforms down to the shop for pick up on Wednesdays, so they can take them to be cleaned. They'll give you a canvas laundry bag to put them in, with your name and the shop's name and address on it."

I glanced at him again, and he seemed to be amused with what I was telling him. "What?" I finally asked.

"Oh nothing," he said, smiling. "Please, continue."

"What are you smiling at?" I asked, nervously. "You're making me self-conscious. Is there something on my face? In my teeth? What?" By that time, he really was laughing at me.

"Nothing, Zoey, I swear," he replied, still laughing. "It's different seeing you at work than it is seeing you at home. Last night, we were all drinking, and you were relaxed and having a good time. Now, you're all business. It's a big change. That's all."

I shook my head and looked away from him. "If you say so. Let's get your uniforms ordered, so you can get out there and get to work." I needed to get this over with, and get him out of the office, so I continued talking. "Joe will bring your uniforms on Wednesday when he picks up my brothers' laundry bags. Um, it's going to be getting cold outside soon, so do you want long sleeve shirts?"

"Let me ask you a question first, if it's okay. What is the tattoo policy here?"

*Tattoo?*

Suddenly, I was very interested in seeing the tattoo he had. *I love tattoos.* Leg tats, body tats, sleeves, back tats,

tats on the ribcage, and on the sides of the torso were by far my favorite.

"We don't really have a policy, so to speak," I replied. "Can I ask what it's of and where it's at?" He raised an eyebrow. "Will it be seen by customers?" I clarified, so he would stop doing that sexy-as-all-get-out eyebrow-raising thing he did.

One of the last two mechanics actually had a tattoo on his forearm that said 'fuck off.' We figured he got drunk one night, and his friends did it to him. He had a slight drinking problem, so he didn't work out for us.

Andy was wearing black work pants and a black long sleeved button-up work shirt, with the sleeves rolled up to a few inches below his elbows. "Yeah," he replied. "They're on my arms, but you can only see them if I wear short sleeved shirts."

*They? There's more than one?* Oh, God, I really wanted to see his tattoos!

"Fine, let's see them then," I said, silently hoping I would get to see all of them. "I am sure they are fine, unless they say something like *fuck off* or are prison tats, but since we've done a pre-employment background check on you, I know you haven't been in prison."

He chuckled and shook his head. "Nope, no prison tattoos for me, and they definitely don't say fuck off." He tried to roll his sleeves up further, but they wouldn't go over his elbows. He slowly unbuttoned his shirt and took the whole thing off instead. He watched me the entire time he was undoing the buttons and taking his damn shirt off, and I *knew* he was totally fucking with me.

He was seriously taunting me with a shirt striptease. Evil man!

*Damn, he's wearing a black T-shirt under the button up. I can't see anything but arms. Oh, but what fine arms they are...*

Holy hell, this dude is ripped. I was finally looking at those muscular biceps I was so fortunate enough to grab hold of at the store. I realized then, he'd been wearing long sleeves every time I'd seen him.

"Well, here they are," he said, smiling deviously. "As you can see, I have no prison tats and no bad language."

He turned his arm back and forth, letting me easily see the whole tattoo. I gawked at his biceps, and he had what appeared to be solid black tribal tattoos, but not the typical American type. They were a series of bold designs, intermingled with fine, intricate patterns. They were amazing and unlike anything I had ever seen.

He seemed to notice I was intrigued, so he lifted his shirtsleeve all the way to his shoulder, where he had a large Tiki looking face tattooed with its mouth open wide and its tongue hanging out.

*Hmm, that's different, but so freaking sexy on him.*

"Tribal?" I asked, a little bit in shock at the situation unfolding in front of me. *This is definitely not what I was expecting when I got out of bed this morning. It was much, much better.*

I reached out and ran my fingertips over one of his tats. He smiled at me, showing his perfect white teeth. *Yep, that made me blush.* "Sorry." I was embarrassed, so I quickly pulled my hand away.

He obviously knew I liked what I was seeing. "I don't mind...at all," he responded softly.

I continued my inspection, without touching, of course. "What do they mean?"

"They're Maori tribal tattoos. I had them done in En Zed," he explained. "I spent about six months there shortly after my divorce. I hadn't been back since we'd moved to the States. I have a house near Auckland that my friend and his wife live in, so I went back to visit them and decided to stay for a while."

The next thing I know, he'd pulled his other sleeve up to his shoulder, showing he had just as many tattoos on that arm. Like his other arm, they encircled the entire bicep. I wondered if they traveled over his shoulders and onto his back and chest.

"Seen enough?" he asked a little provocatively.

*Um, no. Not really.* I felt the heat rising up my neck and onto my cheeks. My mind said no, but my mouth said, "Um, yeah. I think that'll do. Short sleeves it is, unless you want long sleeves for winter, of course."

Andy thought about it for a second, and then decided short sleeves would be fine. He pulled his other shirt back on and buttoned it up. *Darn.* I could've sat and inspected every tiny detail of his tattoos all day long.

"Okay then," I said as I tried to get his tattoos off my mind. "Time to order your pants!" I declared, slightly ruffled, and really wanting to change the subject. "What size do you need?"

He started laughing hard at that point. "What? I don't get to strip down to my underwear for this?" he asked between laughs.

*Now there's an idea... I wonder if he has tattoos on his legs too...*

I realized then that he was totally screwing with me.

"You are such a shithead!" I grumbled as I wadded up a piece of paper and threw it at him, hitting him on the chest. Yeah, it bounced right off. His chest was probably as muscular as his biceps, and most likely covered in tattoos too.

"I need thirty-six by thirty-six pants, please, Zoey," he stated after he finally stopped laughing.

"Jeez, how tall are you?"

"Six-three. How tall are you?" he asked with a sarcastic grin on his face. He was toying with me again.

I wrote down the size he needed and looked away from the order form to find him grinning at me once again. "I am five-eight," I answered, and then quickly moved on. "I think we're done here for now. I'll get this faxed over in a minute and—"

Hearing a sound behind me, I glanced back and saw my mom coming through the door.

"Hey, Mom," I said, and then I introduced her to Andy. She carried a cardboard box in her hands, with two drink holders full of coffee cups in it. I would recognize that blue lid anywhere. She brought everyone coffee from Dutch Bros.

"Mom, you are a saint!" I took the box from her and set it on the desk.

She turned to Andy. "Andy, will you do me a favor and go to the white truck out front and get the pink box from the back seat?"

"Absolutely," he replied happily. "I'll be right back."

I carefully pulled the drink holders out of the box, set them on the desk, and found my coffee. I took a nice long drink of it and collapsed on my chair.

"You made my day, Mom," I groaned blissfully and began to take another drink.

"So, Zoey, why didn't you tell me our Andy was so handsome?"

*Our* Andy? I inhaled at that moment and choked on my coffee, spitting it all over the place. She laughed as she smacked me on the back to try to help my coughing fit. After she stopped hitting me, she mopped up my coffee spray with a paper towel, while I tried to clean myself up and continued to choke. *Fuck, I think it's in my lungs.*

By the time I finished coughing and was able speak again, Andy was coming back into the office, carrying a pink box I immediately recognized from Burrell's Bakery.

He set the box on the desk and turned to leave. "See you later, ladies. I'd better go find something to work on. Don't want boss lady here firing me on the first day." He jokingly pointed his finger at me and laughed.

My mom laughed at his comment. *Traitor!*

"Wait a sec, Andy," she said to him as he turned toward the door. "I brought you a coffee, and this box is full of pastries from the bakery. You'd better get what you want out of there before my boys find out I brought it. Otherwise, you won't get anything."

"Mom's right. They're pigs. In fact, you better take two, just in case." I opened the box and hunted down a chocolate chip scone.

Andy seemed surprised by my mom's kindness to him. "Thank you very much, Mrs. James. I really appreciate everything your family has done with the apartment and the job. It means a lot to me, and I can never thank you enough. Will you let me know how much everything cost for the apartment, so I can repay you?"

My mom looked up at him; she was smiling and shaking her head. He was at least a foot taller than she was. "You are very welcome, Andy, but there is no need to repay us. It was only a little paint and extra furniture.

We're happy you're here, and please, call me Luisa. There's no need for formalities with all this testosterone running amuck. Zoey and I are like one of the boys around here."

Andy thanked her again as he picked up a napkin and took two pastries from the box like I told him to. He took a giant cinnamon roll and the other chocolate chip scone. That guy sure could pack in the food, but you would never know it as fit and muscular as he seemed to be.

Once my mom picked her pastry out, I stood and pushed the intercom button on the office wall to call my brothers in from the shop. "Hey, asshats, there's coffee and a box from Burrell's in here. Come get it."

Through the window, I watched them drop the tools they were holding and run toward the office like a bunch of five year olds. Fearing for my safety, I sat back down on my chair out of the way. "You might want to back away from the box, you two."

My brothers grabbed their coffees and left only crumbs in the pastry box. After thanking our mom and giving her sticky kisses on the cheek, they went back out to the shop, taking Andy with them.

For the next couple of hours, my mom and I worked in peace, catching up on paperwork and taking an occasional phone call. I decided to walk to The Speed Shop next door to see how the morning was going there.

# Chapter Ten

Business was running smoothly at the store, so I went home for a quick lunch, and then drove across town for my hair appointment. Autumn sat me down at her station, where she draped a black cape around my shoulders and lap.

"Long time no see, Zoey. Where have you been?"

"Nowhere really, I've just been super busy. Business at the shop is going well, and so is my store, so it's been keeping me on my toes."

I didn't want to give out too much information. You know how salons are hot spots for local gossip. Word had yet to get out about what Rob had done to me months before, and I wanted to keep it that way.

Autumn took out her scissors and a comb, and laid them on the workstation below the mirror. "So, what are we gonna go with your hair today, girl?"

Wanting a noticeable change, we decided to go with long layers all over, so I would be able to flat iron it, leave it wavy, or flip the ends a bit for a different style.

My hair hadn't been cut in months, so it was all one length and very boring.

After deciding on the style for my hair, Autumn suggested adding some highlights. I trusted her completely and let her do what she wanted. She brushed in platinum highlights where my new chin-length layers would soon be and added more highlights all over to give my golden-blonde hair a sun-kissed look.

The color needed to sit on my hair for a while, so I picked a magazine off the rack and flipped through it. I stopped flipping pages when I came across my favorite cologne ad featuring Paul Walker. It was even the ad with the scent sample, and I immediately thought of Andy.

I hoped everything was going smoothly at work for him on his first day. He seemed to get along well with my brothers, which was a plus.

Looking back down at my magazine, I caught sight of my fingernails and wondered if I could get a mani-pedi while I was at the salon. I checked at the front desk and made an appointment to get my nails done after my hair. I sent my mom a text, letting her know I was going to be a while longer at the salon. About ten minutes passed before I got a response back from her, telling me to take my time and that she had everything under control.

Autumn came over after her timer went off and checked my highlights. They were ready to come out of their foil wrappers, so she began pulling them out of my hair, and each time she did, she would smile excitedly and say, "Stunning!" She was thrilled, and I was getting excited to see it myself.

Next, she washed and then cut my hair. After there was a large pile of hair on the floor from my haircut, Autumn used a flat-iron to style my new cut. When she was finished, she spun me around in the chair to face the mirror.

"Well, what do you think? You've got some serious *ba-bow* going on now, girl!" Autumn said enthusiastically as she continued to arrange my hair around my shoulders.

Assuming that the word *ba-bow* was a good thing, I inspected myself in the mirror. She was right. I looked completely different. Aside from the slightly dark circles under my eyes, I almost resembled my old self.

"Wow! I love it!" I said excitedly. "The highlights made such a difference. Thanks for convincing me to do it, and I love the cut and style." I was thrilled with my new look and tipped Autumn generously for working her magic on me.

It was time for my mani-pedi, so I picked out a fire engine red nail polish, and then slipped off my shoes and socks. The nail tech, Mai, rolled my jeans up to my knees, and I silently thanked God I'd shaved my legs.

While my feet soaked in the warm, scented water, in the whirlpool footbath, Mai worked on my manicure. After she shaped my nails, she painted them, so it didn't take long at all. While my nails dried, she massaged, scrubbed, and did a sea salt treatment on my feet. It felt wonderful, but the sea salt scrub tickled my feet like crazy.

She painted my toes to match my fingernails. When she was finished, I felt completely pampered, but it was time to get back to work

On my way home, I made a stop at the lock shop to have my lobby and apartment keys duplicated, so I could give them to Andy. That way he had access to my laundry room if I wasn't home when he needed it, especially while I was in Cabo for a month and wouldn't be there to let him in.

By the time I arrived back at the shop, it was closing time. I parked at my apartment and went inside the store to see how the day went without me there.

We were so fortunate we hired great employees; I never needed to worry about anything with them there. That was reassuring since I would be gone on my vacation soon. My dad would be around to help if he was needed, so it made me feel better that he'd finally filled the fifth mechanic position. At least he wouldn't be expected to work at the shop and the store.

I headed across the courtyard and parking area, and then through the back door of the shop. As soon as I turned the corner from the hallway into the shop, Noah and Jeremy spotted me and whistled.

"Hey now, you jackasses behave yourselves. We don't want the newbie to start acting like you two when a pretty lady enters the building."

*Did I just call myself pretty?*

My new hair and nails must have helped boost my confidence a little. I peeked around, attempting to be inconspicuous, while trying to see where Andy was.

"He's in the machine shop with Dad, if you're looking for the newbie," Noah teased, tormenting me on purpose.

"Well, I wasn't looking for him, so wipe that stupid-ass look off your face!" I lied, embarrassed at having been caught. My jerk brothers busted up laughing and began putting their tools away for the night.

Once the shop was closed for the day, I headed back home after helping close the store too. I hadn't seen Andy while I was at the shop, since he had been with my dad.

After hanging up my jacket in my closet, I decided to show off my new pedicure, so I kicked off my shoes and socks. *Not that anyone was going to see it besides me, of course.*

It was a bit chilly, so I cranked up the heater and changed into a pair of black fleece lounge pants and a black top. I went to the kitchen to heat up some leftover mac and cheese and fixed a salad to go with it.

While I was waiting for the mac and cheese to cook, my home phone rang. I made the mistake of not checking the caller ID before I answered.

"Zoey, can I come over and talk to you?" a male voice asked. It was Rob. *Shit.*

I let out an irritated sigh. "Talk about what, Rob? We have nothing to say to each other."

I almost hung up on him, but he started talking again. "Zoey, I miss you and want us to try again. I want back everything we lost."

*Is he kidding me right now?* "Rob, that's never gonna happen. *Ever*," I said in an attempt to get my point across.

"Are you fucking that guy I saw you with?" he asked.

*I wish. Holy crap, Zoey!*

After I pushed my initial reaction from my head, I decided that Rob's question pissed me off. It was none of his business who I was, or in this case, was *not* fucking.

"Please tell me why you think that is any of your business, Rob. You need to stop calling here and hanging up too. I know you're calling, because I can see it on my caller ID. Leave me alone!" I growled and hung up on him.

Not even five seconds passed before my phone was ringing again. I didn't answer. He called back three more times, and I ignored those as well. About five minutes later, my phone rang again. I was even more irritated at that point, so I grabbed it and hit the talk button without looking at the caller ID.

"What the fuck do you want from me?" I hissed into the phone.

"Zoey, it's Andy. Are you okay?"

Fuck. I really needed to start checking the caller ID every time my phone rang.

"Andy, I'm so sorry. Rob is bothering me, and I thought he was calling again. Wait, why are you calling my home phone? How did you get my number?" He didn't answer. "Andy, are you still there?" I began to wonder if our call disconnected.

"Yes, I'm here," he replied. "I got your number from the emergency contact list you gave me at work today. I don't like that he's bugging you. Did I make it worse with what I did at the store?"

I didn't want to talk about it over the phone, and I was hungry after my long day. "Can you come over, please? I have something for you anyway."

He took in a deep breath and let it out. "See you in a few minutes."

As soon as he rang downstairs, I buzzed him in and left my front door propped open. While he made his way up the stairs, I flipped on my iPod dock to play some music and sat on the couch to wait for him. Andy came through the door and locked it behind him, turning the deadbolt too. He had changed out of the clothes he wore to work, and was now wearing a T-shirt and jeans. He kicked off his shoes and came into the living room.

As soon as I saw the expression on his face, I lost it. He looked miserable and guilt ridden, not that he had reason to be. He did nothing wrong. He was only trying to protect me. Right then, I knew one thing...I hated seeing him upset, especially when it involved me.

My eyes welled with tears. He noticed I was upset, took both of my hands, and pulled me off the couch into his arms. I couldn't help it, I wrapped my arms around him tightly and cried.

I was frustrated, tired of the phone calls from Rob, and still upset about all the crap he caused all those months ago. Now, when I was finally trying to get over it, he was starting back up again. I wasn't sure if I could deal with it this time.

"Zoey," Andy whispered quietly as he squeezed me a little tighter. "Please don't cry."

I was shaking like a leaf, but I was so relieved to be in his arms. *Why does this feel so easy and natural with him?*

"I'm so, so sorry. All of this is my fault. Please tell me how to fix it," he said.

I pulled back from him, surprised he was blaming himself. "Andy, this is not your fault," I said looking him in the eyes. "It's what he does sometimes, especially if he finds out I'm seeing someone. He's done it before, but since I haven't dated anyone in months, I haven't heard from him."

He sighed and stared down at the floor. "But it is my fault. I'm the one who told him you'd moved on with me, when you haven't." I noticed his accent was more pronounced when he was worried.

Pulling back from him further, I forced him to look at me. I reached up and gently took his face in my hands. The stubble on his jaw was soft, yet prickly at the same time. Why did I feel the need to touch him every chance I got? All I wanted to do now was pull his face down to mine and kiss him. With the way his eyes flashed from my eyes to my lips, I was certain he wanted to kiss me too.

However, it was time to convince him this was all on Rob, as he had done with me the day before. Rob was the one with the issues, not either of us. "This isn't your fault. It's all on him. He is the one who is being an asshole. Please, can we forget about this for now? I want to go lie down for a while."

I was so over the situation and just wanted to go to sleep to forget about everything for a while. I had been having a great day, until Rob ruined it. I wiped away the tears that started drying on my cheeks and then rested my hands on Andy's chest, because he still hadn't let go of me.

"Alright, I'll do whatever you want," he replied with a sigh.

*God he smells good.* He obviously just stepped out of the shower before he called me. I did not want him to leave. I wanted to lie down, but I was still hungry. *Fuck!* I hated it when my brain went all haywire on me. I wanted to eat dinner one minute, sleep the next, and being upset just fucked up my thoughts even worse.

"Did you eat dinner yet?

He shook his head. "No, I was going to fix something and tried your cell to see if I could make you dinner at my place, but it went to voicemail. Your lights were on, so that's why I called your home phone. I wanted to make sure you ate dinner. You're too thin."

"Too thin, huh?"

"Yes, you are," he stated seriously. "You need to eat more and take better care of yourself."

He was right about that part; I did need to take better care of myself. I linked my arm through his and led him to the kitchen, where I pulled out a barstool at the counter for him to sit.

"Let me fix you something to eat then. I was fixing my dinner when he started calling, so I haven't eaten yet either. I'm having leftover mac and cheese and salad. Is that okay with you?"

"Yes, that sounds good. Thank you."

I dumped the mac and cheese from my plate back into the bigger bowl, covered it with a paper towel, and stuck the whole thing in the microwave to heat up. After dishing up Andy's salad, I put it in the dining room on the table next to mine, and then took a seat next to him. I situated my elbows on the counter and rested my chin on my hands, letting out a long sigh.

He moved his barstool closer to me, and then laid his hand on my shoulder to get my attention. "Zoey, I really am sorry about this."

Reaching up, I patted his hand that was resting on my shoulder. "Thank you. You still have no reason to be sorry, but I'm glad you're here. I know we've only known each other a few days, but I really do appreciate you trying to help without judging me."

I stood, wrapped my arms around his shoulders, and hugged him. He swiveled his seat toward me, and then pulled me closer so I was standing between his thighs. His arms wrapped tightly around my waist. The warmth from his body against my cool skin comforted me, and my body tingled in anticipation.

Anticipation of what, I did not know, but the heat was coming off him in waves as his thick, muscular thighs tightened against my hips. His movement pulled me even further under whatever spell he had on me.

Just as he brushed his soft lips across my bare collarbone and laid his head in the crook of my neck, the microwave chimed, letting us know our food was ready. I didn't want to move. I wanted to stay wrapped in his arms. He was warm, strong, and made me feel completely safe and a lot less lonely.

Of course, Will and Justin were right next door, but they came as a pair, so I felt like a third wheel at times. Andy had nobody, and I was by myself. My family lived all over the city. I wondered if Andy needed me as much as I seemed to need him, since his aunt and uncle were the only family he had left.

We released each other, and he picked up the potholders from the counter and pulled the mac and cheese out of the microwave. While he took the food into the dining room, I grabbed the salad dressing and fixed us drinks. We ate in an easy silence.

When all the dishes were washed and dried, we moved into the living room and sat on the couch, not saying anything. It was still early, and I knew I wasn't going to be able to sleep anyway if I went to lie down.

Remembering that I had keys made for him, I pulled them out of my purse and handed them to him. "For when you need to get in here and I'm not home."

"You're giving me keys to your place?" he asked, surprised.

I nodded. "Yeah, I'm pretty sure I can trust you with them since I *do* have all your confidential information in our shop files now. You know, your social security number, copy of your driver's license...all that stuff," I said in an attempt to make a joke. "Besides, I've done a background check on you. You seem pretty harmless."

"You got that right," he said with a smile.

Not feeling like listening to music anymore, I stood up and turned it off, then put on a DVD to watch. I wanted to curl up and relax, watching something mindless. I also wanted to be near Andy, so I sat right next to him on the couch. I put my feet on the coffee table and crossed my ankles.

I remembered him kicking his shoes off when he came in, but I hadn't noticed he was barefoot. He stretched his long legs out under the table and crossed his ankles. I was not a foot person, but the dude even had nice feet. I should not have been surprised, of course, every other part of him was gorgeous from what I could tell.

It was relaxing to sit and not have to talk about anything.

After a long while, Andy spoke. "By the way, I like what you've done with your hair. You look even more beautiful."

I blushed and looked over at him. "Thank you, but I'm not feeling so beautiful right now."

He turned toward me. "Zoey, you really don't see how beautiful you are, inside and out. Look at everything you've done for me, without even knowing me. Who does that? You are sweet, smart, sexy as hell, and you need to try to realize it. Stop letting that asshole bring you down."

No man had ever complimented me before, so I honestly didn't know how to take it. "I'm sorry, I don't know what to say," I admitted. "Thank you for the compliments. I will try harder not to let him get to me."

He simply nodded once, as if saying he was fine with that, and then we both turned back to the movie and enjoyed our silence.

# Chapter Eleven

The silence didn't last for long. About thirty minutes later, the alarm downstairs in the store started blaring.

"What the hell!" I muttered as I leapt off the couch then ran to my bedroom to slip on a pair of shoes. By the time I made it back to the living room, Andy was gone. I grabbed my cell and the keys to the store, and then I ran out the door, nearly running over Will and Justin. They were going downstairs to see what was going on.

Even though I was slightly freaked out, I laughed at Justin. He was carrying a golf club in his hand for protection. Not being the most sports minded person in the building, I took the club from him, because he would probably only hurt himself with it. I would have better luck swinging it than him.

We came around the front corner of the store and found Andy standing at the entrance. One of the doors was shattered, and the glass from it glittered all over the ground, reflecting from the lights overhead.

*Fuck!* I knew exactly who did it.

We didn't find anybody around, so we sent Will and Justin home with their golf club and waited for the cops to show up. When they did show, I let them inside the store to look around. They found a brick laying several feet inside the door.

He threw a brick through my fucking door! The cops took the brick and wrote up a report of the damages. I gave them Rob's name and other pertinent information so they could question him.

Andy and I went into the back warehouse and found a piece of plywood to cover the hole in the door, just temporarily until I could call a glass company to come and fix it. After resetting the alarm, we went back to my apartment.

As soon as we were through the door, I turned to Andy, who was looking extremely angry at that moment. "Can we not talk about this until tomorrow please? I just want to go to bed." I shut off the DVD player and the TV.

"Sure, but you're not staying here alone tonight after this. He might come back. I'll sleep on the couch."

"Oh no, that's not necessary. Besides, my couch is awful to sleep on. Trust me, you wouldn't be able to function tomorrow if you slept on it."

He shook his head. I could tell he was really irritated and didn't want to leave. "No way, you are not staying here by yourself. I'm not risking your safety, Zoey. I'll sleep on the floor then."

He was angry, and I wasn't going to argue with him. However, I wasn't going to let him sleep on the hardwood floor either, and I didn't have a bed in the second bedroom.

"Fine," I said as I grabbed his hand. "You can't sleep on the couch, and you are definitely not sleeping on the hard floor." I pulled him down the hallway and into my bedroom. "Here you go. You can use my room, and I'll sleep on the couch since I'm used to sleeping on it." I took one of the pillows from my bed and a blanket, and then tried to go back to the living room.

He blocked the doorway. "No. I am not taking your bed. We'll both sleep here, but you better try real hard to keep your hands off of me," he joked, grinning wickedly.

We both laughed.

"Have I told you you're a smartass?"

"A smartass, no...but a shithead *and* an ass...yes, you may have mentioned those at least once. Why are you so mean to me?" he teased.

He smiled at me and then he freaking pouted. It was adorable, and I couldn't stop myself from laughing again.

*Silly man, doesn't he know girls are mean to boys they like? Shit... Don't go there, Zoey. We're not in fourth grade.*

I threw my pillow and blanket back on the bed, grabbed my pajamas from my dresser drawer, then went into my bathroom to change. I was too tired to argue with him, and he was definitely not taking no for an answer.

After I washed off my makeup and brushed my teeth, the realization that Andy and I were actually going to be sleeping in the same bed made me very anxious.

*Oh crap, I cannot go back out there! Am I seriously going to sleep in the same bed with him? This cannot be a good idea. I've known him for three whole days!*

Yet, for some reason, I trusted him completely, and I knew he wouldn't try anything. If he did, I was fucked, because I knew I would let him. It had been far too long since a man had touched me. I knew if *he* did, it would be all over for me.

When I finally gathered enough courage to go back into my bedroom, he was already in my bed, with the covers pulled up to his ribs. Andy had tattoos all across his chest and over his shoulders, just as I had hoped.

Holy fucking hell. I needed to shut off the damn lights. His jeans and T-shirt sat folded neatly on my dresser, so I knew he wasn't wearing much under the blankets. *Shit, I cannot do this!*

"Zoey, are you coming to bed, or are you going to stand there all night?"

I didn't say anything. I quickly went over and flipped off the light. Oh yes, much better.

*Now I can't see him. However, I can still feel him there. Fuck! What am I doing? This is crazy. Ah, shit, my eyes are adjusting to the dark and I can see him now.*

I walked around the foot of the bed and slipped under the covers next to him. As soon as I was comfortable and started to relax, my phone rang. I sighed loudly, knowing exactly who it was.

The phone was on the nightstand on Andy's side of the bed. Even as tempting as it was, I was not about to crawl over the top of him to answer it myself.

Andy answered it. "Hello?" He waited a few seconds for a response. "Hello? Is anyone there?" He clicked off the phone and put it back on the charger. Neither one of us said anything for several minutes.

"Goodnight, Zoey."

"Goodnight, Andy."

I felt like calling out goodnight to John-Boy, but I wasn't sure if Andy ever watched The Walton's on TV, so I kept my mouth shut.

There was no way I was going to be able to sleep with him there. Luckily, for me, I was wrong. As soon as I closed my eyes, I was out cold. Similar to the previous nights, though, I didn't sleep more than about two hours without waking.

I rolled over to face Andy, but his back was to me. In the rush to get the visual of him in my bed out of my mind, I forgot to pull the curtains closed before getting into bed, so the floodlights from the shop were letting quite a bit of light in my room.

Instead of staring at my boring ceiling or walls, I stared at Andy's back. It was also covered with tattoos like his arms and chest, and *definitely* a much better view than my walls. The tattoos stretched all across his broad, muscular shoulders and down his back.

Of course, my curiosity got the better of me, so I reached out to move the blanket to see how far down his back they went. I barely moved the blanket when he stirred. I quickly pulled my hand back, praying I hadn't woken him. His breathing became heavy again, and I could tell he was asleep.

I pulled my covers back up and closed my eyes again. I slept longer this time, but a bad dream woke me. I didn't remember what it was about, but when I woke, I realized I had moved closer to Andy. *Much* closer to Andy. My entire body was pressed against his, my head was on his pillow, and my arm was wrapped around him.

*What in the hell? I have lost my freaking mind!*

Not only could I not keep my hands off him while I was awake, I couldn't keep them off him while I was asleep either.

*Fan-fucking-tastic!* I was definitely going out to sleep on the couch!

Very carefully, I moved backward, slowly pulling my arm off him, once again, praying I didn't wake him. Too late, he was awake. I almost had my arm back to myself, when he caught my hand and pulled my arm back around him.

"Stay," he groaned sleepily. He raised his elbow just enough to cradle my arm beneath his so it rested on his side. Andy kissed my hand and fell back to sleep with it clutched in his.

I didn't try to move away again. Frankly, I didn't want to, so I snuggled closer to him. I fell asleep like that and did not wake again until the morning.

When my alarm went off, I tossed the blankets off me and rolled over to hit the snooze button. Andy rolled over behind me, resting his head on my pillow.

"Good morning," he murmured lazily, smoothing my hair down with his hand. *Perfect, I have bedhead.* I am sure he still looked gorgeous.

He pulled the blankets back over us and placed his big hand on my hip. The heat from his hand radiated through my shorts, warming my skin. I was beginning to freak out about where this may be headed. *I cannot do this. He works for my dad.*

"Andy," I whispered. "What are we doing?"

"I'm not sure what you mean, Zoey."

I rolled onto my back, which caused his hand to slide across my lower stomach to my other hipbone. Every nerve ending in my body suddenly ignited. He left his hand there. *Holy shit.*

"Talk to me," he said quietly.

I didn't even know how to start the conversation, so I said nothing.

"Look, I think I know what you're gonna say. Correct me if I'm wrong, but there is some sort of connection here between us, right?" He was staring at me intently, and I knew he wasn't going to let me off the hook. He wanted answers.

Unable to deny my attraction or lie to him, I simply nodded.

"I think we should go with the flow and see what happens," he said with a hint of hope in his voice.

His fingers started tracing tiny figure eights on my belly. I felt all the blood rush through my body and pool about six inches away from where his hand was moving. I was having a hard time concentrating with him touching me. I wanted to agree with him so badly, but I knew I couldn't.

"I can't do this with you. I'm sorry," I said with so much regret that it physically hurt.

His hand stilled on my stomach, and then he pulled it away. My body instantly missed his touch.

"Why not?" He sat up to look at me while waiting for my answer.

I couldn't even look him in the eyes. I sat up too and hugged my knees to my chest.

"You work for my dad," I finally said. "This can't happen between us. I'm sorry, but we can only be friends."

He propped himself up on his elbow and waited for me to say something, but I couldn't speak. I felt like a bitch.

"Right, then. I get it now."

He got out of my bed, wearing nothing but black boxer briefs, and got dressed.

"See you at work later," he said. Then he was gone.

I wanted to call him back, to tell him to strip back down and make me forget all about Rob and the reasons why there could never be anything between us.

I was so fucked.

# Chapter Twelve

There was no way in hell I was stepping foot in the shop after that. I would work at the store all day. I felt horrible about what had happened and could not face Andy. My stomach was in knots, and I was getting a stress headache.

Admittedly, we both felt the undeniable connection between us, but I was so opposed to being anything other than his friend, it was making me physically and mentally sick.

All because of Rob.

Of all the freaking reasons to push someone away. Rob made my life a living hell while we were married, and he was still doing it years after our divorce.

With all of my issues, Andy never stood a chance. What was I supposed to do? He worked for my dad, and I was not breaking my rule.

Would I be willing to see where things went with him if he didn't work for my dad? Hell yes, I would.

That morning, I made calls to the window and door company, who came out and fixed the door quickly. I called our security company, and they came and installed new security cameras all over the building. The inside and the outside of the store now had video surveillance all around for protection.

I also asked the security technician to move the video recorder to the second bedroom in my apartment, so it wasn't inside the store. I did not want to risk someone stealing the security footage to cover their tracks if they broke in.

After finishing with the security tech, I went back inside to find my very anxious dad waiting for me.

"Zoey, what happened?"

We went into the office, and I told him everything. And I do mean everything; from the incident with Rob at Target, to the calls, and obviously, the brick through the door. I also told him I'd become close with Andy, and that he stayed the night after the brick incident, because he didn't want to leave me alone in case Rob came back.

"Dad, I'm sorry. I feel like this is all my fault. I told Andy this morning that we could only be friends."

He put his hand up to prevent me from going any further. "Zoey, do you like him as more than a friend?"

It felt like I was literally about to break. I nodded, and then immediately started to cry.

"Dad, why does this have to be so hard? Why does Rob ruin everything?" I sobbed and plucked a tissue from the box on my desk and dried my eyes.

"Because you're *letting* him, baby girl," my dad stated as he rested his forearms on the desk. "You can't let him control your life. It's time to do what you want. You deserve to be happy, and I cannot stand to see you like this anymore. You haven't dated anyone in who knows how long, you don't go out with your friends, you barely leave your apartment, and all you do is work."

He paused and took a breath, and I could tell he was getting angry. He continued, "It's no way to live your life, and if you found someone you want to spend time with, then you should do it. You can't live your life in the past, Zoey. You, of all people, should know that."

I remained quiet while I let his words sink in. In the end, I still refused.

"I just can't, Dad. He works for you. I will not drag this family into anymore shit like what happened with Rob. He could have really screwed everything up for you and the shop. I don't care what he did to me, but if you had lost the shop because of me, I'd never forgive myself." I wiped my eyes again with the tissue.

"Zoey, he's nothing like Rob, and you know it," he stated matter-of-factly. "Don't even compare the two of them. I realize we haven't known Andy very long, but you know how you get a gut feeling about people? Well, he is a good person according to my gut. He's already fitting in like one of the family over there," he said, pointing toward the shop.

I was happy to hear that, but I didn't want to tell my dad that what he said only made it worse. Andy fit in over at the shop, and my dad needed him. The last three mechanics, including Rob, had been useless. My mind knew I shouldn't risk it, but my heart said differently. I was determined to listen to my mind.

"Think about it, baby girl. You have my blessing if you want to date him. I don't like seeing you so lonely all the time." He hugged me and left.

Business was a little slow after lunch, so we took our time and restocked the shelves in the store. I noticed I really needed to do inventory, so I placed a few orders, and then checked out front in the store to see if anyone needed any help.

We had no customers in the store at the time, so I met with our three employees: Jerry, Tara, and Josh. I let them know what happened to the door and that extra security cameras had been installed. I asked them to keep an eye out for Rob and to let me know if they noticed anything, or anyone, suspicious around the store.

They were very understanding and concerned for my safety, and they held no judgment at all over the whole situation. I also let them know there was a new mechanic next door, so they would be seeing him around. I showed them Andy's picture on my phone, so they knew what he looked like until I could introduce him to them. He would be at the store occasionally to pick up parts and other items he needed for the shop.

When four-thirty rolled around, I decided to stop working for the day. I went upstairs to my apartment, changed in to my pajamas, and climbed into my bed. I rested my head on the pillow Andy had slept on the previous night. It still smelled like him. I couldn't get away from him, even in my own apartment.

Sleep continued to evade me, even after I laid there for nearly an hour trying to take a nap. My mind was wandering through everything that had transpired that morning and my conversation with my dad.

Frustrated, I rolled over and faced the windows that overlooked the back of the shop. My brothers were outside at the back of Andy's shiny, black, enclosed car trailer, lowering the door ramp down. It appeared that they'd stopped working for the day but stayed after to check out Andy's car.

A few minutes later, a flat-black colored '69 Camaro slowly started rolling backward down the ramp. Once it was off the ramp, they pushed it forward a bit and unhooked the winch cable from underneath. Andy came out of the trailer, hopped into the car, and fired up the engine.

I dragged myself out of bed, changed back into my clothes, and pulled a James Racing sweatshirt over my head to go next door to the shop. I wanted to check out the Camaro, but I also wanted to see *him*. I could not stand it any longer and needed to know if he was mad at me.

When I arrived in the parking area, I found the car trailer closed and locked. The guys and the Camaro were gone. I began to wonder where they had gone so quickly, but then I heard the unmistakable sound of the dyno bay door rolling up on the other side of the shop. It had an ear-piercing squeal to it when it was rolling up, so I waited outside until the door stopped moving.

After I entered the shop, I made my way to the dyno bay windows. Our customers loved the fact they could watch the mechanics run their cars on the dyno. It was a 'man thing', according to Jeremy, and something I wouldn't understand.

From the outside of the dyno bay, I observed through the window as my dad showed Andy how to hook up the dyno to his car and then how to work the machine itself.

Andy eventually glanced over to the window and saw me standing there. He gave me a slight wave and went back to concentrating on what he was doing. I watched as they ran the car through its paces on the dyno machine and made slight adjustments under the hood.

I also couldn't help but notice that the relationship between Andy, Dad, and my brothers was very natural. They talked and acted as if they had known each other for a lot longer than they did. My dad was right. Andy was already fitting in with my family. I was very attracted to him, but could I risk everything all over again?

My stomach started to rumble, so I waved goodbye and headed home. I wasn't even sure if anyone noticed me leave.

That night was the first dance class with Jess and Sasha, so I needed to go home to eat and change my clothes. Thank God Jess had sent me a text earlier to remind me, because I had forgotten about it. Because I didn't feel like cooking anything, I fixed a cold sandwich for dinner.

I made a mental note to stop at the store on the way home from class to pick up a few groceries I needed. I didn't know I would be grocery shopping with Andy the weekend before, so I hadn't taken my list when we went shopping.

My fridge and pantry were reminding me of the movie *Friday*. I had peanut butter, but no jelly; Kool-Aid, but no sugar; and ham, but no burger. I chuckled to myself at my *Friday* comparisons and finished my dry sandwich.

For class, I pulled on some stretchy, black yoga pants I could dance easily in and a black tank top. Luckily, we were having a warm winter in Nor Cal, so I would not freeze my ass off. We'd barely had any rain this year, and it wasn't too cold yet.

Since I hadn't asked Jess, I was clueless as to what dance we were learning. Honestly, I didn't even care, because I decided I needed to get out more. I was feeling lonely being by myself at the apartment all the time. I had her sign me up to get me out of my apartment, so I was going to the damn class!

At that point, I was just happy that each night for the rest of the week, I had something planned to keep myself busy. My only free day was going to be Sunday.

I pulled my hair back into a ponytail, put on a jacket, and left.

# Chapter Thirteen

I found the address for the class and went inside the dance studio, where Jess and Sasha were already waiting for me. I paid the fee for the class at the front desk, and then went over to say hello to my friends.

"Zoey!" Sasha screeched. "Oh, my God! It feels like I haven't seen you in ages." She hugged me tightly and lifted me off the ground, even though she was shorter than I was.

"Sash, can't breathe," I managed to gasp out while being squeezed to death.

"Oh, sorry, Z," she replied with no hint of a real apology in her tone. "I've missed you. By the way, you look like shit. I think I just cracked your ribs, you're so skinny."

Leave it to Sasha to tell me the truth...and why was everyone picking on my weight? Did I look that bad?

I chuckled when I realized Sasha hadn't cracked any ribs, but she had popped several vertebrae in my back, which in turn, began to ease the tension in my muscles. That felt nice.

"Thanks, Sasha. Tell me how you really feel," I muttered.

"You know I love you, Z, and that's *why* I said it. How much weight have you lost? You have dark circles under your eyes, too. Are you not sleeping well?"

I felt like we were playing a game of Twenty Questions. I wasn't offended; I loved her honesty, and I needed to hear everything she told me. "You know me too well," I admitted. "It's been a rough few days." *Rough few days, my ass...it's been a rough few years...*

Right then, the instructor called the class to order. I leaned over to Jess and whispered, "What dance did you sign us up for anyway?"

She smiled sweetly, but I noticed the sneaky gleam in her eyes. "You'll see..."

*This can't be good.*

The instructor greeted us loudly as she stepped in front of the class. "Ladies, my name is Jane. Thank you for joining me tonight."

Jane was tall and willowy; definitely a dancer. She was wearing what I thought was a black cat suit, so she almost looked like a dominatrix. I fully expected her to be carrying a whip.

"Welcome to Seductive Dance!" she announced as her eyes wandered over the group of us standing in front of her.

Holy fucking shit.

My jaw dropped, and I glared over at Jess, who was bouncing up and down with excitement. She feigned innocence and shrugged her shoulders at me while batting her big brown eyes.

That little shit. I guess next time I'd better ask before agreeing so easily. What did I get myself in to now?

I said yes to Jess so easily about the class. Why couldn't I agree with Andy so easily? He wanted to take things a day at a time to see where it went. Why was it so hard for me to do that? It's not as if he would purposely do anything to hurt me. I hadn't known him very long, but I instinctively knew it wasn't something he would do.

Sasha elbowed me in the ribs to get my attention. "Ouch, you whore!" I growled. "That hurt!"

She smiled and poked me hard in the ribs, so I slapped her on the butt and then yanked her hair.

"Oh, Z, when did you get to be such a kinky bitch?" she joked. "You smack my ass and pull my hair. What are you gonna do next, whip me?"

I had to cover my mouth to hide a laugh after her comment. It had begun to look like a scene from a Three Stooges movie, and I was fully prepared to block an eye poke from someone.

We missed Jane's entire opening speech because of our shenanigans. I glanced around the studio and silently cheered because there were no stripper poles in sight. I swore that if I found out our dominatrix dance teacher had a whip somewhere in the vicinity, Sasha would get her ass whipped with it.

Jane asked us to take a chair and line up in rows. She was teaching us dance moves as if we were actually performing a dance for someone sitting on a chair. I guess, for me, it was fitting to be doing a lap dance with an empty chair, since I didn't have a man and had pushed away the only one who interested me.

We started out with the basics of learning to do a striptease and lap dance. Aside from that, the class and hanging out with my friends was great. The class was actually a lot different from what I was expecting. It was...fun.

Later on, after we were more comfortable with each other and ourselves, Jane began teaching us a routine to a song. Not caring for the song choice, I let my mind drift and thought of a few other songs on my iPod that would be perfect to practice to at home if I wanted.

*Awesome. I can dance with a chair in the privacy of my own home. I am living the high life.*

Jane encouraged us to embellish our dancing any way we liked. She told the group to do what felt right to us individually, and she assured us there were no wrong moves. She taught us how to incorporate several steps, including seductive walking, body rolls, and hip rolls.

Surprising to me, it was not tacky at all. It gave me a sense of empowerment by the end of the night, and I promised Jess and Sasha that I would continue the class with them.

Now, if I could keep the empowered feeling going in my day-to-day life, I would get myself back on track.

I turned to Jess. "Thanks for not telling me what I was getting into, Jess. I never would have come if I had known. Do I dare ask why you wanted to take this class, though?"

She smiled at me. "Well, since Noah and I have been together for a few years now, I wanted to do something special for him on our honeymoon."

*Oh, this is for my brother's benefit.* "Okay, thanks for the visual." I shuddered, not wanting to picture Noah sitting on a chair straddled by Jess.

He was my brother. I'd seen and heard him acting like a gross boy since I was adopted. I endured the burping and farting contests between him and my other brothers; the smelly gym socks, the whole nine yards.

Regardless of all the gross things I saw him do over the years, I loved him. I was glad Jess loved him enough to want to do things like this for him.

She slugged me lightly on the arm. "Just think, when you find someone, you will be well prepared because of it, so don't complain."

My mind immediately drifted to Andy, and I frowned.

"What's with the look, Z?" Sasha questioned.

"I'm pretty sure I ran off the only guy who is ninety-nine percent perfect for me," I stated miserably.

"You met a guy? Where? When? Zoey, we need to talk about this. *Now!*" Jess was beginning to throw a fit.

They each grabbed one of my arms and dragged me to a coffee shop down the street. When we bought our coffees and found a table to sit at, they forced me to speak.

I explained what all had happened with Andy since we met. I told them about our amazing connection. I told them how easy it was to talk to him, and how hard it was for either of us to be around each other without touching. I seriously could not keep my hands off him, and vice versa.

"Z, you said he's ninety-nine percent perfect. What's the one percent that is not perfect?" Sasha probed. "From what I'm hearing, this is a match made in heaven."

"He works for my dad. That's the problem." I took a drink of my coffee and set the cup back down on the table.

Both of my friends were dumbfounded, not understanding *why* that was a problem. I hadn't told them about Rob suing me, so I had to go back and explain all of that too.

"That dirty rat bastard!" Jess growled when I was finished telling them what happened. "I knew something happened, but Noah wouldn't tell me anything. Zoey Lynn James," she scolded. "You should have come to us. We would have been there for you, but you shut us out."

"I know. I'm sorry," I said regretfully. I felt like a terrible friend. "I wanted it to be over and done with, so I could forget about it."

Yet, here it all was again, front and center, right where it didn't need to be. Fuck, this whole freaking situation sucked. My emotions and thoughts were all over the place. I could not make a rational decision if I tried.

One thing I knew for certain, I wanted Andy. Badly. But I couldn't have him. In just a few short days, he had flipped my already fucked up world upside down.

Sasha sat and listened the whole time I was talking without saying a word. Suddenly, she blurted out, "Let's go find Rob and kick his ass!" causing Jess and I to burst out laughing.

I was grateful she lightened the mood. It did feel good to get the Rob saga out in the open, too. It felt like the weight was starting to lift a bit.

"What are you going to do about Andy, Z?" Sasha asked.

I shrugged. "There's nothing I can do. I won't go down that road again since he works for my dad. If I did date him, and it ended badly, it would be uncomfortable for Andy and everyone else at work. If he didn't work there, we wouldn't be having this conversation."

"Tell your dad to fire him then," Sasha said bluntly.

I frowned at her. "Very funny, Sash. He fits in perfectly at the shop with my dad and the boys. I'll deal with it somehow."

*How long can I deal with it?* It felt like my heart had literally dropped from my chest when he walked out this morning.

Why was he having this effect on me? I would never know, because I was never going to be anything other than friends with him. I couldn't risk it...*again.*

We sat and talked about my upcoming vacation while we drank our coffees, and they decided to take a week off from work and go to Cabo with me. It was getting late, and I still needed to stop at the grocery store. I realized I forgot to turn my cell back on after class, so I pulled it out of my purse and powered it back up.

I had missed a few calls and had three new voicemails. I scrolled through the calls. There were two from Andy and one from Will. I listened to the messages. The first two were from Andy.

*"Zoey, where are you? It's getting late, and you didn't tell anyone where you were going. I'm getting worried. Please call me, so I know you're alright."*

The second message was similar.

*"Zoey, it's me again. Please call me when you get this. I don't care how late it is."*

What the heck? Was something wrong at the store again?

My phone automatically advanced to the third message. It was from Will. He left it less than ten minutes before I turned on my phone.

"Hey, Zoey-girl, your boy Andy is worried about you. He thinks something is wrong. Please tell me you are not avoiding that sexy hunk's calls. Honey, please call him a-sap. Love ya, baby girl."

Jess and Sasha watched me impatiently as I listened to the messages. Once I listened to them, I told my friends what was going on, and they made me play one on speaker so they could hear Andy's voice.

"Oh my," Sasha said, resting her hand over her heart. "Would you listen to his accent?"

I think she literally swooned. I know I did every time I heard his voice.

When I showed them the picture he took of himself on my phone, she pretended to faint. I rolled my eyes at her and laughed. Freaking drama queen.

"Guess I'd better call him back," I said.

"Maybe you should pull your head outta your ass too, while you're at it," Sasha muttered before she took a sip of her coffee. I flipped her off, and she smiled sweetly in return.

First, I sent a text to Will, letting him know where I was. When I called Andy, his phone barely made it through an entire ring before he answered.

"Zoey, where are you? Are you alright?"

"Hey," I replied. "I'm fine. My phone was shut off while I was in class, and I just remembered to turn it back on. Sorry if I worried you."

He sighed with relief. "Alright, I was feeling uneasy because of all the crap going on. Where are you?"

"I'm having coffee with my friends, Jess and Sasha, now, but I'm heading to the store to pick up a few groceries. Do you need me to get anything for you while I'm there?"

"I don't need anything, but please be careful. It's late. Will you call me when you get home, so I know you're safe, please?"

I agreed, and we ended our call.

"I better get going, before he sends out the search party," I said with a hint of sarcasm, yet secretly loving the fact that he cared enough to be worried about me.

"Z, don't push him away," Jess whispered when she hugged me goodbye.

Once I left the dance studio where my car was parked, I drove over to the store and found the items I needed. I decided to stroll down the alcohol aisle to see if anything tasty was on sale. It wasn't on sale, but I picked up a bottle of Johnnie Walker and put it in my basket. I had taken a liking to it since Andy brought a bottle over. I paid for my groceries, and then headed toward my silent apartment.

After turning onto my street, I noticed my Chevelle sitting on a side street a few blocks from my apartment. Rob was sitting inside the car. Was he seriously waiting for me to come home? Fuck!

As soon as I drove past him, I heard the car start and the headlights came on. *Shit.*

Not taking my eyes off the road, I dug through my purse, found my cell, and called the closest person I could think of...Andy. I could have called Will or Justin, but Rob knew them, and they wouldn't intimidate him as much as Andy would.

He answered his phone on the first ring again.

"Can you meet me out in my parking space right now? Rob is following me. I'm almost home." I tried not to sound scared, but I heard my own voice tremble with every word I spoke.

"I'm on my way outside right now. Stay on the phone with me until you get here. I swear I won't let him hurt you, Zoey."

I heard him shuffling around, most likely putting on his shoes. His door slammed and I heard him breathing as he went down his stairs. In the next few seconds, it sounded like he was jogging.

I glanced in the rearview mirror again, and Rob was still behind me, but a few hundred feet back.

"Andy, he's still behind me." Why was he following me? *This is not good.*

"Don't worry, Beautiful. I'm right here waiting for you. Just keep moving. I can see you coming down the street. I'm not going anywhere," he promised.

He had already opened the gate, just enough for me to drive my Audi through, so I pulled into my parking space. We hung up our phones, and he shut the gate behind me.

Andy opened my door for me and helped me out of the car. I wanted to fling myself into his arms and never let him go, but I didn't... I couldn't.

We were pulling my grocery bags out of the trunk, when I heard the Chevelle slowly approaching outside the fence. I caught the unmistakable whining sound of the gear drive in the motor Jason built for the car and the kick-ass exhaust system that Jeremy custom built with Flowmaster mufflers.

No other car in the world sounded as sweet as my Chevelle. I missed my car.

We waited to see what Rob was going to do, but fortunately, he sped off. There was no nasty confrontation like at the store over the weekend. Thank God.

"C'mon, let's get upstairs," Andy muttered. I knew he was mad.

Andy could be mad all he wanted, but I was livid, so I took out my cell and called Rob.

"What's up, babe?" he asked arrogantly. "Did you miss me?"

What a douche. "Look, you piece of shit," I growled into the phone. "You need to leave me the fuck alone, or I'm going to get a restraining order."

He scoffed. "Whatever you say, babe," he said and hung up on me. *Wow.*

Along with my purse, I carried a grocery bag upstairs as Andy carried the other two bags for me. We made it inside my apartment and set the bags on the kitchen counter. Saying nothing, we started putting everything away.

Andy pulled the Johnnie Walker out of the bag, took two glasses out of the cupboard, and poured us each a drink. I hopped onto the counter to sit, and he slid one of the drinks across the countertop to me.

After I downed it in one gulp, he poured me another. I swallowed the next one just as fast.

"Thank you for calling me when you noticed him, Zoey."

He poured a third drink for me. *Yep, I am beginning to feel pretty warm and brave now.* Thank you, Johnnie Walker. I pulled off my jacket and tossed it onto the back of the barstool.

"Andy, about this morning," I said quietly, knowing we needed to talk about the situation we found ourselves in. I owed him an explanation. "I'm sorry, and I need to explain what my issues are."

He nodded in agreement. "Yes, I think you do." He came to stand in front of me and took a long swallow of his drink.

While thinking of what I should say, I gulped down my third drink. I had no clue what to tell him. "I'm sorry. I'm having a hard time trying to figure out what to say and how to say it." I held out my glass to him. "Can you pour me another one please?"

He took the bottle off the counter from behind him and poured me another. "Liquid courage?" he asked. I nodded, because I needed all the help I could get with this conversation. "I guess I don't understand what the issue is, Zoey."

I swallowed the last of my drink, and it burned all the way down. I put the glass down, and Andy rested his hands on the countertop on either side of my knees. He was standing so close, and he smelled so good. I could feel the heat and frustration that radiated off his body. I wanted to wrap my arms and legs around him and kiss him until I couldn't feel anything but him. But I couldn't...

*Focus, Zoey. Focus.*

"You work for my dad," I blurted out. "*He* worked for my dad while we were together and after we split up," I stated, pointing toward where Rob had just been outside.

Andy moved back a step and put his hands up defensively. "I'm not him, Zoey. I feel like you're taking what he did out on me."

That was not what I was trying to do. I shook my head.

"Please don't think that. You are definitely nothing like him, and I know that. As I was saying, you work for my dad. What if we try this and it doesn't work out between us? Where would that leave my dad and the shop? I cannot do that to him again. He could have lost everything he'd worked his whole life for...because of *me* and my shitty decisions."

I hoped Andy understood why I was doing what I was doing.

"I should be going, then," he spoke, devoid of emotion.

Oh, God, no. My stomach dropped, and every fiber of my body ached. "Andy, I'm sorry. Trust me that this is hurting me too, but we can only be friends."

He appeared disappointed and shrugged his shoulders, without a doubt, giving up on us. "Okay, friends it is. It's better than nothing."

Andy turned and walked away from me. When he got to the front door, he stopped. "Goodnight, Zoey." A second later, he was gone.

He was hurt, and I understood why. He must have felt like I was leading him on when I let him stay the night with me and he woke up with me draped over him. I would need to be careful when I was around him, or try to avoid him altogether. I hated it, but it would be better that way.

The four glasses of Johnnie Walker I had guzzled were kicking in. Andy left the rest of his on the countertop, so I picked it up and drank it too. *Maybe at least I'll sleep tonight.*

When I was in bed, I pulled the covers to my chin and turned onto my side, so I was facing the back of the shop, and Andy's apartment. My apartment was in a much older building, built in the early twenties. It had several massive windows around the entire upper floor of the building. The windows were each the size of double doors and easily seven feet tall, so I had an open view of the shop and apartment next door.

Lying there staring out the window, I could see the lights on at Andy's. Occasionally, I would see him walk by one of his windows, and I wondered if he was feeling as horrible as I was.

Unable to sleep, I got up and sat in the antique chair facing one of the windows that overlooked the courtyard below. I rested my feet on the edge of the wide windowsill. I used to love to sit in the chair and read, but I hadn't done it in ages.

Andy's door swung open and he walked out of his apartment onto the landing at the top of his stairs. He leaned on the railing with his arms folded across his broad chest, facing me. The floodlights on the back of the shop were bright enough, so I could see him clearly. He was looking right at the window where I was sitting. I wasn't sure if he could see me or not, and I really didn't mind if he could.

I sat in my chair and watched him until I couldn't stand it anymore. I was going to give myself an ulcer if I did not stop stressing. I finally stood and went back to bed.

As soon as I laid down and pulled up my covers, Andy turned around and walked back inside his place. A minute later, his lights went out. I then knew he was able to see me, and he had waited until I went to bed before he did.

# Chapter Fourteen

The next day, I avoided the shop at all costs. We were busy at the store, so I barely saw Andy at all, and when I did, it was from a distance. His uniforms arrived that morning, and when he returned from his lunch break, he was wearing one. He looked gorgeous in it too.

Thankfully, I finished out my day at work without incident. We'd gotten so busy I was actually running late to rehearsal for the anniversary party.

Luckily, I hit traffic just right and made it on time. I met with Ben and the band, and we ran through the song list. We worked on the songs that I was going to be singing lead vocals. It felt great to be singing again, and in no time, I felt comfortable being back on a stage.

The couple who was having the anniversary party had picked great songs for us to perform. They chose a mix of modern rock, pop, and even threw some hair bands into the mix. I would be singing lead vocals on songs by Madonna, Pat Benatar, and Joan Jett. In addition to singing lead and backup vocals, I would be performing several duets with Ben.

We finished rehearsal around eleven that night. Ben promised Friday's rehearsal was going to be brief since we accomplished so much. I was leaving when Ben called after me, so I stopped and let him catch up.

"Zoey, do you still talk to Sasha at all?"

I nodded and grinned slyly, because I knew where the conversation was headed. "Yes, we go to a class together, so I see her twice a week." Sasha had lusted after Ben all through high school. "Ben, if you're interested in Sasha, you should call her. I'm sure she'd love to hear from you."

He perked up. "Really? You think so? She would never give me the time of day back in high school."

Ha! He must not have tried very hard. Men. I gave Ben her phone number and headed home.

By the time I arrived at home, I was exhausted. I hadn't had even two minutes to myself all day. Once I was ready for bed, I stood at my window and stared across the courtyard at Andy's place. All the lights were out so he had already gone to bed.

The day had been pure torture for me. Even though I was busy, I could not get my mind off *him*. I wondered if he was still upset with me, or if he realized why a relationship would never work out for us. I knew that tomorrow I would need to work over at the shop part of the day. I was dreading it and looking forward to it at the same time.

Fortunately, the next day was much the same. We were busy all day long, which was fine, because I barely saw Andy. He popped into the office for a minute to say 'hi,' and went back to work. It was awkward, and I literally felt the frustration and tension between us. It left me with a sick feeling in my stomach and an achy heart.

He was trying to be my friend, just as I'd asked. I wasn't sure how long I could stand to be in the same building so close to him, so I decided I better get my work done quickly, and then get the hell out of there.

I hadn't picked up the mail since Monday, so I had a good-sized stack to sort out. I went about my normal routine of opening everything first, then organized it into a few different piles. I shredded the junk mail, arranged the new magazines on the table in the lounge, and then sat down with a pile of bills and bank statements.

I pulled a bank statement out of its envelope and scanned over it, my eyes stopped suddenly when I saw the account balance at the bottom of the page. *What in the hell?* The balance was over seven hundred and fifty thousand dollars.

I scanned over it again and realized I had made a huge mistake. The bank statement did not belong to us. It was addressed to Andrew J. Tate. *Shit.* The mail carrier had put it in the wrong box, and I failed to notice the forwarding address sticker on the front of the envelope.

Several thoughts passed through my mind at that point. The main one being, why did he have so much money? *None of my business.* I folded up the statement and stuffed it back in the envelope. I then checked the rest of the mail to make sure I hadn't opened any more of his by mistake.

*Shit!* I needed to let him know what I had done. I stood and peeked out the window to the shop. He looked like he was in the middle of something, so I sent him a text.

*Can you come to the office when you get a minute? No hurry.*

About ten minutes later, he poked his head through the open door.

"You needed me, Zoey?"

*More than I ever imagined,* I thought. I knew I was falling for him, hard, and it saddened me to be near him. Regardless, I needed to tell him what I did, so I asked him to come in and shut the door.

"Did I do something wrong?"

"Have a seat," I said anxiously, so I could get the conversation over with. "You didn't do anything wrong, but I accidentally did, and it affects you. I need to tell you about it."

He leaned forward, resting his elbow on the corner of the desk. "Should I be worried?" he asked, suddenly very serious.

Setting the envelope on the desk, I pushed it toward him. "I'm so sorry. This was in the shop mailbox by mistake. I opened it and looked at it before I noticed it didn't belong to us."

He picked it up to see what it was. A wave of relief washed over his face, and he actually laughed. "Jesus, Zoey. I thought you were gonna tell me something bad."

*Oh, he's not mad. Good.* "I thought you'd be upset." I sighed with relief. "I'm sorry. I go through the mail and open everything first without looking at it. It's from the same bank we use, so I didn't notice it wasn't ours until I saw the balance."

He ran his hand up his face through his stubble, and then briefly pinched two fingers over the bridge of his nose where his scar was.

"Zoey, it's no big deal. I'm not upset about you seeing this at all. It's my mum and dad's life insurance money."

That made sense, but I still felt bad about opening it. "I'm still sorry. It is none of my business how much money you have, or why. Forgive me?"

"There's nothing to forgive," he said in an irritated tone. "It's fine, really. At least you know I'm not interested in you for your store or money now, right? I have more than enough money of my own, trust me."

Ouch, that hurt.

He stood and stalked toward the door to leave. My mouth dropped open, and I sat back in my chair. His comment went straight to my heart. *Does he really think that's why I told him no?*

"Andy, I'm sorry if that's what you thought..." My voice wavered, and he was instantly back at my side.

"Zoey, I'm so sorry I said that. It was uncalled for, but there are things you don't know about me too. I've had people do shitty things to me, but it's not going to stop me from trying to make a life and be happy. Too much has been taken away from me already."

His voice dropped to a whisper as he spoke, and he took a seat in the chair next to the desk. Andy gently took hold of my hand and rubbed his thumb back and forth across my fingers. "It's not going to keep me from falling in love with someone who makes me happy."

What was he saying? Did he mean me? *Oh God, this has to end.* Now.

"Andy, stop!" I pulled my hand from his, stood, and began pacing around the office. "I can't do this. It's hard enough as it is, but having to deal with it all here...at work—"

The office door flew open, and Jeremy barged in. "What the fuck is going on in here?" he demanded, glaring at Andy.

He pointed at Andy then turned to me. "Is he giving you shit, Zoey?"

I shook my head. "No, he's not. I'm fine." *I am going to throw up.*

Jeremy stepped toward me protectively, blocking my view of Andy. "I don't think you're fine, Zoey. I walk by, you're in here, obviously upset, and you seem to be arguing with *him* about something. Now tell me what the fuck's going on," he growled.

Shit, he was really getting pissed.

Jeremy had always been my main protector. He'd stepped in between Rob and me several times when we fought at the shop. He had no reason to step between me and Andy, so I moved to the side so I could see him again.

"Jeremy, you're misunderstanding what you saw," I said firmly, putting my hands up in defense.

I refused to tell him the truth, because if I knew my brother, he would start treating Andy differently. It was the last thing we needed at the shop. *Again...*

Andy started to stand and say something to Jeremy, but I shot him a look, begging him not to, so he sat back down. I went to Andy and took the bank statement envelope from his hand.

"Jeremy, it's not what you think. We were talking about this." I waved the envelope back and forth at him to show him proof of what Andy and I were originally discussing. That is, before the shit hit the fan and we began arguing about our personal lives, or lack thereof.

I wasn't going to show him what was inside, because it wasn't mine to show, but I needed to do something.

"I accidentally opened his mail because it was in our box my mistake. I felt bad, and he was only trying to convince me it was okay, because I was freaking out about it. It's no big deal, I swear."

Andy narrowed his eyes at me, probably trying to figure out why I was lying to Jeremy. It's not like I was really lying about it, I just wasn't telling him the whole truth.

He must have realized why, because after a minute he stood and took the envelope from me, pulled out the statement, and handed it to Jeremy.

"Read it," he told my brother. "She thought I'd be upset with her for opening it and seeing I have some money."

Jeremy flipped through the papers. When he came to the bottom of the page where the account balance was, he was surprised and confused, just as I had been when I saw it.

"It's my parents' life insurance money," Andy said. "They died over ten years ago."

Jeremy folded the papers and put them back in the envelope. "I'm sorry for your loss," he said sincerely to Andy as he handed the envelope back to him.

Andy gave him a curt nod. "Thanks."

"Sorry I freaked out on you guys," Jeremy told us. "I did get the wrong idea. I thought you were arguing, and after all the shit Rob pulled here..."

I breathed a sigh of relief when he stopped talking. I didn't want him to go on about Rob.

"Okay, okay, we get it," I muttered. "We're good, here. Right, Andy?"

He nodded and looked away. "Yeah, sure...we're perfect."

Jeremy backed up toward the door. "You need to chill, Zoey. Don't get so worked up about shit you have no control over. It was an accident that you opened the envelope. Like you said, it's no big deal."

I smirked. "Sure thing, Jer. I'll try harder next time to *chill*."

He left the room, shutting the door behind him and leaving Andy and me alone in the office. "We didn't need to lie to him, Zoey," Andy said the second the door clicked shut.

"Please, don't," I begged. "This is why there can't be anything between us. What happened right now is exactly the type of situation I wanted to avoid." I dropped down onto my chair. "We aren't even together, and we get in one little argument, and my brother sees it and flips out."

He reached over and squeezed my hand. "I'm sorry about what I said earlier, Zoey. I know where you're coming from, though. I know what it's like to have something that makes people want to take advantage of you."

He stood, folded the envelope, and stuffed it into his back pocket. "Someday, I hope you'll trust me. *You* are all I want. Nothing else," he stated frankly.

*Holy crap.*

"I'd better get back to work. The boss lady might get mad at me for taking such a long break," he said with a grin, his blue eyes teasing me. He turned and walked out the door, leaving me sitting alone in the office, trying to pick my jaw up off the floor.

After dinner that evening, I rushed off to the dance studio to meet Jess and Sasha. We had a great time in class again. We were familiar with the dance steps and the instructor, so we were able to get through the routine several times.

Sasha was being a hyper little shit and forced me to sit on her chair while she gave me a lap dance. She said she wanted a real person to practice on, since she was single too. I'm not sure if she was trying to cheer me up, or herself, because of our severe lack of male companionship. She even had Jane laughing at her crazy antics, and a couple of the other women in the class threw dollar bills at her.

At the end of the night, Jane told us that for our next class, we would be learning a different routine and dance. She also told us that during Christmas break and the week after New Year's, there would be no class. The class would go right up until my friends and I left for Cabo.

After I gathered my purse and jacket, I said my goodbyes to Jess and Sasha, and then headed home. I watched the roads near my apartment for Rob again. He was nowhere near my place, from what I could see, and that made me relax.

As soon as I was safely inside, I showered and slipped into some pajamas. I checked my phone before I went to bed, and found a text from Andy.

*Text me back so I know you made it home.*

Well that was straight and to the point. I sent him a reply that was a little nicer than the text I had gotten from him.

*I'm home, goodnight.*

A few minutes later, my phone pinged with another text from him.

*Goodnight, Beautiful. Sleep well.*

That man was going to break my heart, and he would never even know it. No matter what happened between us earlier in the day, he was still on my side, and still trying to protect me.

I hated it, but I knew I needed to distance myself from him even more after the incident that morning, especially after what Jeremy had seen. I would not let it happen again. Maybe I would sneak over after hours and work. It would be better for everyone if I worked less at the shop while Andy was there.

# Chapter Fifteen

The next few days passed by in a blur because I kept myself overly busy and avoided the shop during business hours. To me, there was no other choice if I was going to keep my sanity.

The night of the anniversary party, I did my hair and makeup so that it looked like I was going out for a night on the town. I slipped on my little black dress, a jacket, and my black four-inch heels. After one last look in the mirror, I grabbed my purse and left.

When I arrived at the party, it was already in full swing. I found Ben and the rest of the band, and he introduced me to the couple who was throwing the party. They offered us a hefty cash tip if we would stay an extra hour and play songs their friends and family requested.

I couldn't refuse. I needed a night out, and some of the guys in the band needed the extra cash.

The couple hired a DJ to play music before and during their dinner and drink hour. They scheduled us to perform from nine to ten-thirty, but because of the change, we would be playing until eleven-thirty. Knowing that Andy would probably worry, I sent him a text before we went on stage, letting him know I was going to be home later than I originally planned.

I hadn't seen or talked to him since that day in the office, but he already knew from a previous conversation what time I would be home. It was easier to tell him I would be home later, because I just didn't have the heart to worry him.

Whether I wanted him to be or not, he was my silent keeper.

The band gathered backstage, I stowed my purse and jacket, and we headed out to perform. We went through our entire song list, and the crowd danced and cheered loudly for us between songs. I was having a great time on stage, singing and dancing along with the music.

I hadn't had that much fun, or felt so relaxed, in a very long time. It was nice to let all of my personal issues go for a while and do something that I loved.

At ten-fifteen, Ben let the crowd know we would be taking song requests for an hour when we returned from a quick break. They went wild cheering again. Backstage, I sipped a bottle of water and checked my phone, finding a new text from Andy.

*Thanks for letting me know. I appreciate it. Enjoy the party.*

We went back out on stage, and the crowd called out several song requests to us. I ended up singing lead vocals on the majority of the songs. They requested everything including The Go Go's, Blondie, and more Madonna songs. Eleven-thirty rolled around, and we finished on stage, thanking the crowd. By the time we finished talking with guests and said our goodbyes to the anniversary couple, it was well after midnight.

The guys and I walked out together and I hopped in my car to leave. I scrolled to my Snow Patrol playlist, hoping they would help me unwind on the forty-five minute drive back home. I was exhausted by the time I pulled through the gates and into my parking space. It had been a long and draining week for me. The party made it more exhausting, and I wanted to crawl into bed and sleep for two days.

Andy's apartment was dark. His truck was in his parking space, so I knew he was home.

As soon as I secured the lobby door, I reached down, took off my heels, and went upstairs. I set my purse and keys down on the table beside the door and headed toward my bedroom.

As I entered the hallway, I noticed the television was on in my dark bedroom. I didn't remember having it on that day. When I abruptly stopped, I heard the buzzer on my dryer go off, indicating a load of laundry was dry. *Andy.*

I tiptoed down the hallway and found Andy on my bed, fully clothed, except for his shoes of course. I knew they would be sitting by the front door. He was lying on top of the covers sound asleep, and an infomercial was playing on the television, the volume muted.

On the floor next to my bed was a basket full of clean, folded clothes. I'd given him the key so he could do his laundry, and that's what he was doing. I wasn't sure why he was asleep on my bed, though. He looked so peaceful while he slept, so I decided not to wake him. I stole a T-shirt from the stack of clothes in his laundry basket and tiptoed out to the hallway bathroom to get ready for bed.

After I shed my dress and bra, I slipped Andy's dark blue T-shirt over my head. It had the words 'New Zealand' across the front in faded white lettering. It was an old shirt and was super soft, having been washed hundreds of times. I loved it, and I loved how it smelled like him.

When I returned to my bedroom, I found Andy still asleep. He must be exhausted too, if he's fallen asleep on my bed while doing his laundry. It made me sad that he waited to do it until he knew I would be gone for hours. After what I did to him, it was a good way to avoid me. I couldn't blame him, though. I'd avoid me too if I were him.

Ever so carefully, I eased into my bed and pulled up the covers. Andy didn't stir. Silently, I watched him sleep and enjoyed the scent of his cologne. My eyelids were getting heavier, so I clicked off the television with the remote and set it on my nightstand.

Andy stirred, and his eyes fluttered open. I had woken him up.

"Hey, sorry I woke you."

"Hi. I guess I'd better go home, eh?"

I shook my head. "It's late, Andy. You can stay if you want to."

He seemed tired, like he hadn't been sleeping well.

"I was doing my laundry and fell asleep on the couch. You were right. Your couch sucks to sleep on," he mumbled sleepily as he closed his eyes. "I came in here to wait, instead. I hope you don't mind."

"I don't mind at all. Go back to sleep."

Without saying another word, he drifted off again. I wanted nothing more than to lean over and kiss him goodnight, but instead, I pulled the extra blanket from the foot of the bed and covered him with it. When I was comfortable, I rested my hand on his bare arm and reveled in our skin on skin contact. I slowly descended into dreamland.

When I woke up the next morning, he was gone. The blanket I'd covered him with was folded up and lying on the foot of the bed. It was as if he'd never been there. Only I knew he had been. I was still wearing his shirt.

Over the next week, he avoided me like the plague. Apparently, letting him stay the night was a bad idea. Every time I would see him around the shop, he looked as miserable as I felt.

I didn't try to talk to him and spent as much time at the store as possible instead of the shop. Maybe it was better that way. It certainly didn't feel better, but I would have to get over it.

My mom had let me know she needed me in the office on Friday, but I knew she didn't. She was clearly using it as an excuse to get me over to the shop, since it was my birthday. My family always did something special for me that day.

Friday morning, I arrived at the shop early to find a huge sign on the outside of the back door that read "Happy Birthday, Zoey!" They had also tied balloons to the doorknob. I went inside, and the entire office was decorated pink.

Pink streamers were everywhere, pink helium balloons floated around the ceiling, and pink confetti covered every surface, including my computer keyboard.

I knew Adam was the one to throw confetti all over the place. He was such a shit sometimes. There was also a giant pink box from Burrell's on my desk, which made Adam's mess tolerable. I swiped the confetti off my chair with my hands and sat down. I picked up my keyboard, turned it upside down, and smacked it with my hand a few times, trying to dislodge the confetti from under the keys.

My brothers came barging into the office a minute later and sang...no, *yelled* happy birthday at me. They raided the pastry box and then went to work.

I turned back to my desk, laughing, and began digging around inside the box for my chocolate chip scone. I wondered where Andy was, because he was late to work. I didn't need to wonder for long.

"Happy Birthday, Zoey," he said softly from the doorway behind me. My heart sped up at the sound of the deep, accented voice I had missed hearing for days.

Mentally preparing myself to talk to him for the first time in a week, I took in a deep, calming breath and spun my chair around to face him. "Thank you, Andy." He stepped into the office and held out a large coffee from Dutch Bros.

I thanked him again as I took the coffee from him, and when I did, I noticed he'd written "Happy Birthday!" on the lid. It made me smile.

"How have you been?" I asked, attempting to break the iceberg between us.

"I've been alright, I guess. You?"

I had missed him like crazy. "Same," I replied. He was acting like he had something on his mind, but wasn't sure if he should say anything.

"I'll see you later," he said abruptly and turned and walked out the door.

A split second later, he was back.

"Zoey, do you have plans for your birthday?"

I shook my head. My family wanted to take me to dinner, but I wasn't feeling up to it, and I denied all invites from my friends too.

"Can I take you to dinner?" he asked hesitantly. I must have frowned because he quickly added, "Just as friends, of course. I didn't know it was your birthday until I came downstairs and saw the balloons and sign on the door, so I didn't get you a gift. I hope the coffee is good. It has an extra shot of coconut, just the way you like it."

My heart felt like it would rip out of my chest, and my throat felt like it was closing up. I wanted to go with him. I missed being around him. I missed our easygoing banter back and forth. I missed...him.

"Come on, Zoey..." A mischievous grin lit his face, and I swear, he *sang* the words "just say yes" and started laughing.

The man did know his Snow Patrol, and "Just Say Yes" was one of my favorite songs by them.

Before I knew it, I was saying yes. He smiled, relieved. "Perfect, I'll pick you up at seven."

He turned and left before I changed my mind. I chuckled, because I had a feeling he was going to use those same tactics to his advantage again someday when I told him no. I had a feeling I would let him too.

Throughout the workday, I received several deliveries from my friends and family for my birthday. The staff at The Speed Shop had a giant bouquet of balloons delivered to me. Sasha and Jess had sent an enormous gift basket of chocolate, wine, and all kinds of edible goodies. Most of it was extremely fattening and full of calories. I knew my friends were telling me I was too thin again.

*Bitches.* I loved them for it, regardless.

My mom and dad hand delivered a gorgeous basket made out of dried grapevine, which was overflowing with a grapevine ivy plant. Three of my brothers brought me iTunes gift cards, but Jeremy thought it necessary to buy me a bottle of silver Patron tequila and margarita mix. Great, I was going to be craving margaritas all day.

I went home for lunch and took as many gifts with me as I could carry. I fixed a salad, and then added my gift cards to my iTunes account so I could shop for new music over the weekend. I planned on working at the store the rest of the day, so I headed downstairs after lunch.

Entering the store through the front doors, out of habit, I walked up and down the aisles to see if anything needed restocked on the shelves. The front of the store looked great, so I went to find everyone to thank them for my balloons.

They were all helping customers, so I went to my office to start on some paperwork that I'd been putting off. As soon as I walked through the door, I saw a giant vase filled with at least two dozen red roses sitting on my desk.

I knew instantly who had sent them. During our years together, Rob never got it through his thick skull that I didn't care for cut flowers. To me, they were a waste of money, because as soon as they were cut from the plant, they were dead.

Even though I knew I should've thrown it away without reading it, I read the card.

ZOEY,

*I MISS YOU. PLEASE GIVE ME
ANOTHER CHANCE. HAPPY B-DAY.*

*I LOVE YOU, ROB*

Seriously? All of my friends and family sent me the most beautiful gifts, and I was not going to let his gift ruin my day. He had ruined too many of my days already.

Picking up the flowers, I jogged through the warehouse and out the back door with them. The water from inside the vase sloshed over the rim as I marched across the parking area to where our large dumpster was located. I hurled the entire vase full of roses over the side and heard them crash to the bottom, shattering glass all over the floor of the dumpster.

Guess they just emptied it. Oops.

I turned around, wiped the water off my hands, and began walking toward the store. As I was walking past the back of the shop, I heard someone clapping. I stopped to look around and found Andy standing outside of his apartment door at the top of the stairs. He was clapping at my rose chucking performance. He must have been coming back from his lunch break and saw the entire show.

"Very nice, Zoey," he joked. He had a proud grin on his face. "I give that an eight-point-five."

He was seriously rating my chucking skills. *Too funny.* I decided to go with it and bowed gracefully to him.

"Thank you," I joked back. "I'll be here all day. My next performance will begin shortly." I shook my head and went back to the store.

A while later, my mom called from the shop to tell me I received another delivery. "I'll come get it later, Mom," I said. I was still in the middle of paperwork and didn't want to stop until it was finished.

"Sorry, Mija," she said laughing, "but this delivery has an expiration date on it, so you need to come and get it now."

What in the heck did that mean? Whatever she meant, it definitely had me intrigued. I walked over to the shop and went straight to the office. Everyone was standing at the door, waiting for me with very peculiar expressions on their faces.

They led me down the hallway toward the shop where there was room for all of us. Something big was happening, but I knew it wasn't something bad with the way everyone was grinning. As soon as I walked around the corner and into the shop, the singing began.

Yes, standing in a row directly in front of me was a Barbershop Quartet. Not only was it a Barbershop Quartet, it was a *gay* Barbershop Quartet. I knew the group, because they were friends of Will and Justin's, and I'd seen them perform. They sang a very rousing rendition of "Happy Birthday" to me before handing me a card.

I was in hysterics, with tears running down my face as my family and Andy stood around, clapping at the performance and laughing with me. I opened the card and read it.

*Happy birthday,*
*birthday, birthday,*
*birthday, Zoey!!*

*Love you lots,*
*girlfriend!*

*Love, Will & Justin*

Without a doubt, I had the best friends in the entire world! I cried happy tears as I hugged and profusely thanked the quartet. Hands down, this was the best birthday ever.

Rob's flowers forgotten, I enjoyed the rest of my day at work. I found myself smiling each time I remembered all the sweet things everyone had done for me.

I stayed late, finishing the paperwork at the store, and before I knew it, it was six. I ran upstairs to take a shower and get ready for my birthday dinner.

# Chapter Sixteen

Andy gave no indication of where we were going for dinner, so I decided to pick something a little dressy to wear, just to be on the safe side. I chose a silvery colored, knee-length chiffon tank dress and matching jacket. It was simple, but just a little bit flirty. I set my clothes aside, put on my makeup, and fixed my hair.

Right at seven, Andy knocked on my door. "Hi, come on in. I still need to change." I decided to see what he was wearing first, so I would know if my dress was too much for our dinner.

I was not prepared for what walked through the door a second later. He wore a black, long sleeved, *Affliction* brand, button-up shirt with a gray design on the chest and back, perfectly fitted faded blue jeans, and nice black dress shoes.

I was sure at that point, I started drooling. He'd even trimmed his stubble and styled his short hair. I was definitely wearing the dress after seeing him. Andy took a seat on the couch, while I went and changed into my dress and jacket. I slipped on my favorite black heels and headed back to the living room.

"Ready?" I asked, picking up my purse.

He stood and turned toward me. After a few seconds of him looking me over, he said, "Wow, you look gorgeous."

I smiled and appreciated his compliment. Hey, I was trying. I didn't do so well the last time he complimented me. "Thank you. You're pretty gorgeous yourself." This seriously felt like a date.

He stepped over to me and held his elbow out toward me. "Let's go eat." I slipped my hand in the crook of his arm, and we headed out the door for dinner.

"Where are we going?" I asked as he pulled his truck out of the parking lot.

He sighed, seeming slightly uncomfortable. "Since I don't really know of any restaurants around here, I was hoping you'd tell me where to go. Besides, it's your birthday, and I want to take you someplace you like."

I'd been craving a margarita all day, thanks to Jeremy giving me the tequila, so we went to my favorite Mexican restaurant. They had a full tequila bar and the best margaritas. We were seated in an extremely tiny booth near the back of the restaurant.

I slid in on one side of the U-shaped booth, and Andy slipped in next to me. The waitress asked what we would like to drink. Andy ordered a beer, while I decided what flavor of margarita I wanted.

After I ordered, the waitress asked me for my ID. For some reason, she was somewhat snotty when she asked, but I didn't let it bother me. When she was finished, she set it on the table, instead of handing the ID back to me. Umm, interesting...

Andy picked it up and looked it over. Fortunately, my picture was decent.

"You're twenty four today, eh?" he asked as he handed my ID back to me.

"Yep."

"I didn't realize you were so much younger than me."

I tried to remember, but I couldn't think of what his birth date was from his papers at work. "How old are you?"

"I turned twenty-eight in August," he said. He was the same age as Jeremy, who had just turned twenty-eight in November. That might explain the whole 'protect Zoey' thing they both did.

The waitress delivered our drinks and took our dinner orders. I noticed her paying extra attention and being flirty to Andy while she took his order. Of course, he didn't notice. What was it about women that made them so... Ugh. I wasn't going to think about it. We were only friends, and I had no business getting jealous about anything.

After she left, Andy picked up his beer and held it up for a toast. "Happy birthday, Zoey."

"Thank you," I replied as we clinked our drinks together. I took a long drink of my strawberry margarita after licking a bit of salt from the rim of the glass. It was very strong, but it was good silver tequila, so I didn't care. I hadn't eaten a big lunch, so my stomach was empty, and I knew I should drink it slowly.

We shared a basket of chips and salsa while we talked about our day. The restaurant was loud, being a Friday night, so we were forced to scoot closer together so we could hear each other. It really felt like we were on a date, but I was having a good time, so I relaxed and tried to enjoy my birthday dinner.

My margarita glass was empty when our food arrived, so I ordered another one. Andy stuck with drinking water after his beer was gone, since he was driving.

After we finished dinner, we sat and talked as I drank my second margarita. I was feeling a little tipsy. It had been a great day and was only getting better, since I was spending the last of it with Andy. Our easygoing closeness was back, and we talked about everything other than what was going on, or *not* going on, between us.

The waitress brought our check, Andy slipped his credit card into the black booklet, and she left with it. While we waited for her to return, several people wearing sombreros stopped at the end of our booth. I glanced at Andy, praying they were not going to do what I thought they were.

Yep, they were at the table to sing "Happy Birthday." Someone dropped a giant, glittery, hot pink sombrero on my head, and they sang to me. I was mortified, but too buzzed to care much.

The ringleader of the singers pulled out an old Polaroid camera and asked Andy and I to pose together for a picture. After the picture came out of the camera, Andy and I watched as it developed. Even after two margaritas, I couldn't help but notice how happy the smiling people in the photo looked. Just as I started to get a little emotional, a waiter dropped off a dish of flan with a candle in it.

The photo quickly forgotten, I playfully smacked Andy on the arm. "You didn't ask them to do this, did you? I'm so embarrassed!"

He shook his head as he chuckled. "No. It wasn't me, I swear. You know I've been here the whole time, and I haven't talked to anyone but you."

It must have been the server's idea when she checked my ID. That surprised me with as snotty as she'd been.

Andy pushed my dessert dish in front of me. "Make a wish, Zoey," he said, tipping his head toward my dessert that still had a burning candle in it.

I knew exactly what to wish. I closed my eyes and wished for the strength to overcome my daily struggles and learn to trust people again.

We split the flan for dessert, or should I say, he fed it to me, because I kept dropping my spoon. I guess I was a bit more buzzed than I thought. Andy was obviously amused, because he would not stop laughing and tormenting me.

Every time he would put the spoon near my mouth, and I would go to take the bite, he would pull it away and put it in his own mouth. He went so far as to tell me how delicious it was, and how I should order my own dessert and stop trying to eat his, because he "doesn't like sharing."

After laughing my ass off, I finally jabbed him in his rock hard abs with my finger. He accused me of playing dirty, but then fed me the rest of the flan. I loved the way he stared at me while he fed me my dessert. It was almost as if he enjoyed doing it, and I couldn't help but notice the way his eyes slightly changed color the longer he watched me. I definitely wondered what he was thinking about...

Once we stood to leave the restaurant, the tequila hit me and I swayed a bit before righting myself. As soon as we were at his truck, I was full on drunk. I was a happy drunk, not a sloppy drunk, so it was all good.

I climbed into the truck, not so gracefully, I might add. As I put on my seatbelt, I accidentally dumped the entire contents of my purse down between the seat and the door. *Fuck me!*

Andy jumped in on the driver's side and found me giggling hysterically. "What's so funny, Beautiful?" he asked.

I stopped laughing when he said the word *beautiful*, but only because it surprised me to hear him call me that again.

"Sorry," he said quietly, a hint of sadness in his blue eyes.

"I don't mind. I like it when you call me that. I feel beautiful when I'm with you," I drunkenly confessed. He grinned, and then started the truck.

He drove us back home and parked in his space. After he stepped out of the truck, he came around to open my door. As soon as he pulled the handle, I remembered why I was giggling when he got in the truck at the restaurant.

I tried to grab the door so he couldn't open it, but it was too late. It was already swinging open. The contents from my overturned purse fell out of the truck, landing on his feet and the ground around him.

A surprised expression washed over his face as he glanced down at the balled up receipts, tampons, loose change, and who knows what else. It only made me laugh harder.

"I guess this is what you were laughing at earlier?" he asked as he pointed down at his feet. I nodded and continued laughing.

Shaking his head, Andy grinned as he stepped back and kneeled down to pick up my junk for me.

I hopped out of the truck to help him, and ended up almost falling on him because of my heels. I pulled them off and dropped them inside my purse too. "Fuck me," I muttered. "I need a smaller purse."

"I'll never understand why women need to carry so much shit around," he teased as we continued picking up the *shit* that had fallen out, dumping it back into the black hole I called my purse.

After everything was back in it, we walked toward my place. I stepped on a tiny rock with my bare foot. "Ouch!" I stopped to brush it off, almost falling over in the process, because I was standing on one foot and trying to keep my balance after two very potent margaritas.

"Hop on, drunk girl," Andy joked as he squatted down in front of me. I hopped onto his back and lightly wrapped my arms around his shoulders. With his big hands on the backs of my bare thighs, he effortlessly piggybacked me toward my building.

As he walked, I rested my chin on his shoulder. "Thank you," I whispered in his ear. "This has been the best birthday ever."

Boosting myself up his back a little bit to reach his cheek, I kissed the side of his face. His stubble tickled my nose, causing me to let out a quiet giggle.

He chuckled. "All I did was buy you coffee and dinner."

"It was the best part." I rested my chin back on his shoulder. It felt amazing to be with him after so many days of not seeing him, so I squeezed him a bit tighter.

He stopped at the lobby door and carefully set me down, so I could dig my keys out of my purse. Of course, I couldn't find them since it had been overturned. Andy laughed as he pulled his keys back out of his pocket and unlocked the door.

"Come drink a margarita with me?" I asked and pulled him through the door, not waiting for him to answer. I didn't want my birthday to be over yet, not until midnight anyway. Then I didn't have a choice.

We climbed the stairs to the landing, where he unlocked the door to my apartment. "Wait a sec," I said as I stepped over and knocked on Will and Justin's door.

Justin answered the door, looking tired and wearing only pajama pants. He smiled when he saw Andy and me together outside his door. "Thank you for helping make this the best birthday ever," I mumbled as I hugged him. He hugged me back, and I felt another set of arms around me. It was Will, joining our hug.

"I love you guys," I told them. "Want to come join us for a margarita?" They did and followed us next door.

I set my iPod on shuffle and mixed our drinks. We sat on the couch talking and drinking our margaritas, until a song by Frank Sinatra came on, and Will decided it was time to dance.

He stood up and bowed in front of me. "My lady, a birthday dance?" he asked politely, holding his hand out to me. I took his hand, and he helped me up from the couch to dance with him.

I sort of knew how to dance to that type of music, so I didn't make a complete ass out of myself. I was no Ginger Rogers, but of course, Will was a natural. Halfway through the song, I gave up trying to keep up with him, and pulled Justin off the couch so he would go dance with Will.

They were adorable dancing barefoot in their flannel pajama bottoms.

After the song ended, we did some tequila shots. I was the only one who was drunk, but they were all catching up to me. It felt like the last time the four of us had gotten together for dinner and drinks. The guys did a couple more shots after I decided to quit drinking, so I wouldn't wake up with a hangover. I was having a great time with Andy and my friends.

"Harvest Moon" by Neil Young came on, and the boys went back out to the living room to dance. "Dance with me?" I asked Andy as I held my hand out to him.

He nodded hesitantly, took my hand, and we joined Will and Justin on the makeshift dance floor. The song was upbeat enough for us to dance without it feeling awkward since we were doing the *just friends* thing.

We swayed back and forth to the beat of the music, and Andy very gracefully spun me around a few times, surprising me with his dancing skills. He was really good.

"You really know how to dance, don't you?" I asked inquisitively.

He spun me out to the end of his arm, and then spun me back in, so I was leaning on his chest; one of my arms was behind his back, and my other hand was in his.

"Yeah," he answered, appearing slightly embarrassed. "My mum made my sister and I take lessons when we were young."

I imagined a smaller, younger version of him, dancing at his mother's insistence. It made me sad for him, and all he had lost.

"Dark Roman Wine" by Snow Patrol came on, and I tightened my hold on Andy. We slowed our dancing down to match the tempo of the new song.

"We hate to be party poopers on your birthday," Will said, "but it's been a long week. We're gonna head home."

We told them goodbye and continued dancing. We danced until the song ended and another slow Snow

Patrol song came on, "An Olive Grove Facing the Sea." The lyrics were brilliant, and they forced me to think about what was happening between Andy and me.

I realized the drinks I consumed had completely obliterated all of my defenses, but I wasn't going to fight it. I wanted to savor the moment of the two of us, dancing in my apartment, on my birthday.

My walls were down. I was tired of being weak, and tired of being alone. The perfect man was right there with me, and I was being a complete idiot by pushing him away. Right then, I knew without a doubt, I was falling in love with him. I wanted to tell him, but I was terrified.

As the song played, I felt him tighten his hold on me. I wrapped my arms around his waist and rested my cheek on his broad chest. I squeezed my eyes shut, and breathed him in, letting a tear escape down my cheek. While we slowly swayed, I decided to give in and let go of everything in my head, and not worry about the consequences anymore. I wanted to live in the moment so I made the first move.

My feet stopped shuffling and I took a small step away from Andy. I gazed up at him, and he had a confused expression on his face as he stared back down at me. I placed my palms on his chest while we continued to watch each other. My breath quickened as Andy's demeanor changed from semi-relaxed to tense. I slid my right hand up his chest, and rested my palm on his stubbly jaw.

The way he was looking at me, like he wanted to devour me on the spot, made me want to let him do it. His eyes snapped shut as my hand made its way back down to his chest. He took in a deep breath and let it out when I unbuttoned the top button of his shirt and began on the next button down.

"Zoey, I need to go," he said abruptly, taking my hands in his and backing away from me.

"What?" I asked. "Why?" I wanted him to stay so I could tell him how I felt.

He moved further away from me and buttoned his shirt. "Because," he said with so much frustration and confusion in his voice, I knew he was hurting too. "This is getting too intense, and this fucking song..."

Now I was confused. "I thought you wanted me?"

He took a step back. "I do, Zoey," he admitted. "You have no idea how much. But—"

I cut him off and stared up at him. "But what?"

He shook his head and ran his tongue over his bottom lip, wetting it. "You've had a bit to drink tonight, and when tomorrow comes, I know you're going to shut me out again."

I was speechless. He was probably right, but I didn't *want* him to be right. "I'm sorry," I whispered, letting my arms fall to my sides in defeat.

Leaving him standing there, I turned and made my way toward my bedroom.

"Zoey, stop," he called after me. "Please, come back and talk to me."

He was right, so I kept walking away. As soon as I sobered up and realized what I was thinking, I would regret it. But I didn't want to regret it. I hated the fact that I was hurting him. I was being selfish and was so confused.

As I walked through my bedroom door, I pulled my pretty dress off over my head and tossed it onto the floor. My mind told me that I needed to sleep it off and forget about everything that just transpired between us.

I pulled a drawer open on my dresser, and dug around trying to find something to wear to bed.

"Zoey?" Andy spoke from the doorway of my bedroom. I didn't even bother covering up the bra and panties I was wearing, because I was beyond caring about anything at that moment.

"You're right, Andy," I choked out without even looking at him because I was too ashamed of my behavior. "I'm sorry for being selfish and leading you on. I've had too much to drink tonight, and all the feelings I have for you...they *are* real, but I know tomorrow I will be back to my normal, miserable self. I'm sorry if I hurt you."

Yes, that was me shutting him out again. I knew it, and he knew it. Finally, I glanced in his direction and could barely see him through the tears in my eyes.

"Fuck this!" he muttered angrily. A minute later, I heard my front door slam. He left without saying goodbye, and he was mad.

Unable to hold my emotions in any longer, in one rash decision, I swept everything off the top of my dresser with my hands, hurling it all against the wall. The glass saucer that sat under my orchid plant shattered all over my floor. My orchid plant broke in half and littered the contents of the pot all over me and the floor.

I wrapped my arms around myself and dropped to my knees, crying, my entire body shook from the wracking sobs that emanated from deep within me. So there I sat, half-naked, on the floor, covered in bits of plant, and crying like a fucking baby. *On my fucking birthday.*

I'd officially hit rock bottom, and it hurt like a bitch.

My phone pinged, so I picked it up from where it landed on the floor, amongst broken picture frames and my demolished seashell collection. It was a text from Andy.

*I'm sorry about everything. I don't know how else to get through to you. I want you to say yes to me. I know what a lyric addict you are, so listen to them. Just Say Yes. Please.*

Why was it, in the brief time I'd known him, he got me like nobody else did? He knew how to talk to me. Who else would tell me to listen to the words to a fucking song to make me see what he wanted to say to me, but he couldn't because I kept pushing him away?

Nobody, because they didn't get how my brain worked, but he did...in such a short time, he understood me like no one else ever had.

I picked myself up off the floor and cleaned up the mess I'd made. It was time for me to clean up my life next. I listened to the song he wanted me to, and he was right to send it to me, because the lyrics were perfect. It was simple. I knew it was. I wanted to say yes to him.

After I fell into bed, I laid there with "Just Say Yes" playing on repeat and thought about how miserable I was. Over the last several months, I had systematically pushed everyone I loved away. My family and my friends were all I had, and I'd been treating them like shit.

Now someone new and wonderful had come into my life who made me feel worthy and special, and I did the exact same thing to him. *What the fuck is wrong with me?*

All I was doing was living in the past, exactly like my dad said. I needed to get my shit together before I lost Andy and myself completely. I was already too close to it as it was. I rolled over, gave Andy's apartment one last glance, and for the first time in years, I cried myself to sleep.

# Chapter Seventeen

After a very restless night, I woke after ten the next morning. Even though I drank so much, I remembered everything that had happened the previous night. Nothing changed in my feelings toward Andy. I loved him. I had no doubt.

All I wanted to do right then was fade away into oblivion.

I absolutely hated myself. I hated who I'd become and hated myself for the pain I'd been causing my family, friends, and myself. I was being selfish and needed help, so I was giving myself an intervention before I chickened out. I was being an idiot, and I knew it.

The only way I could do that was to leave, so I could get my life together and come back to him, ready for a relationship. I could not lose him. No, I would not lose him. Not over this.

I had no plan for where I would go...I just needed to go. After pulling my suitcase out of my closet and tossing it onto my bed, I filled it with clothes, and then got ready to leave. I packed my iPod, my laptop, and my purse, and then headed down to my car.

The sight of Andy's truck in the parking lot was a reminder of how horribly things had ended between us the night before. Still, I pushed on. I needed to stay focused.

When I stepped up to my car, I found it covered with the red roses I had tossed into the trash the previous day. *What the fuck?* The rose petals had been ripped from the stems, so it looked like my white car was covered with giant droplets of blood. It was creepy.

Upon closer examination, I noticed my car also had two flat tires. I walked around to the driver's side, and those tires were flat too.

Rob had slashed all the tires on my car. I knew he did it. He must have been watching when I threw the roses away, otherwise he wouldn't have known where they were or that I'd even trashed them. It made me feel uneasy, thinking he might be watching me, and I wondered how often he did it.

Apparently, I wasn't going anywhere right away. I was furious and refused to take his shit anymore. I was to the point of being so mad and frustrated, that all I wanted to do was cry. I held it in and let my anger push back the tears.

I closed my eyes and took a deep breath, then pulled my suitcase over to the shop and let myself in the back door. I dropped my belongings off in the office, went into the shop, and found a floor jack with super low clearance so it would fit under my car with four flat tires.

The jack was heavy for me, but my adrenaline was pumping, so I dragged it out the back door and over to my car. I went back inside the shop, found four jack stands, and had to carry them out two at a time, but I got them all out to my car too.

I turned on the air compressor inside the shop and found enough air hoses to hook together to get an air gun out to my car so I could take off the tires. If my dad taught me one thing to do well, it was to change a fucking tire.

There was no way he was going to let me slide through life, not knowing how to change a tire or the oil in my own car. I could use any piece of equipment inside the shop. Not as well as my brothers, but in a pinch, I could do it if I needed.

I used the floor jack to lift my car, and carefully positioned the jack stands under the front. Once I was satisfied with their placement, I released the floor jack, slowly lowering my car onto the stands. I dragged the jack around to the back of my Audi and did the same thing.

I was on a fucking mission.

Once I jacked all four tires up off the ground, I took them all off my car using the air gun. My adrenaline was pumping like crazy and it was exhilarating. I took the floor jack and the air gun back inside, then picked up my purse and the keys to the shop truck.

I pulled the truck in next to my Audi, dropped the tailgate, and lifted my tires into the bed of the truck. At that point, I was filthy dirty, covered to my elbows in brake dust and road grime, and I couldn't care less. I closed the tailgate, hopped in the truck, and left.

I drove to our friend, Tom's, tire shop, where Tom put four new tires on my wheels. He seemed concerned about the condition of my tires, but he didn't ask what happened. I think he could tell by my mood, *not* to ask. I paid with my credit card and drove back to the shop, where I pulled alongside my car and took the tires out of the truck.

When I looked at my car, I saw that all the roses were gone. *What the...?* I turned back to the shop to go get the floor jack and air gun again.

Andy was coming down the stairs from his apartment. "Rob?" he asked as he motioned to my car.

"Good guess," I muttered as I stalked past him to the shop. I was still pissed, and needed to keep my momentum going.

Andy was waiting for me when I went back outside. "Do you want some help?" he asked hesitantly.

I sighed loudly. "No, thank you. I am perfectly capable of doing it myself."

He chuckled. "Yes, I saw that earlier."

I looked over at him, and he was smirking at me. I glared back. "What?" I growled.

"Oh nothing," he replied with a breath-stealing grin on his face. "You're kind of hot when you're working on your car all pissed off." When my eyes widened in surprise, he laughed and put his hand up. "Let me rephrase that. You're hot all the time, but when you're mad, dirty, and doing what you're doing... it intensifies it."

Seriously? I shot him an irritated glare, and he freaking *winked* at me. I tried to be annoyed with him for saying it, but it was funny, so I laughed instead.

"Thanks a lot, smartass."

He smiled as he sat on the tailgate of the shop truck with his arms crossed over his chest, watching me put the tires back on my car, not offering again to help. I appreciated it. It was almost as if he wanted me to know he was there if I needed help, but I was going to have to ask him for it if I did.

Andy was the only person that understood me well enough to know I needed to do it on my own. Anyone else would have pushed me aside and done it for me.

Yes, I was trying to prove to myself that I could get over what Rob did to my car. Yes, it had cost me several hundred dollars for new tires, but I had taken control of the situation. I was not going to let him get to me anymore. I was done with his shit.

When my tires were back on my car, I lowered it to the ground and dragged everything I took outside, back into the shop. I washed my hands and arms, then collected my suitcase from the office and wheeled it out to my car.

Andy jumped off the tailgate, surprised to see me with my suitcase. "Where are you going?"

"I don't know yet," I admitted. "Just...away." I popped the trunk of my car open and hurled my suitcase inside.

"Are you leaving because of me?" he asked dismally.

"No, I'm leaving because of *me*." I was being honest with him. Everything was my fault, and I needed to fix it. He simply made me realize how fucked up I truly was and how I didn't want to be anymore.

"Please don't go." He walked over to me. He was too close so I backed away a step.

"I need to. I can't be like this anymore." He reached out for me, and I took another step back. I couldn't let him touch me. If he did, I would lose my momentum.

"When are you coming back?" he asked as he shoved his hands into his front pockets.

I shook my head. "I don't know. When I feel better, I guess."

He took another step forward, so I took another step back. I was pressed against my car and unable to back up any farther. I could feel the desperation and concern radiating off him in waves.

"Thank you for cleaning off my car," I said, changing the subject. When he nodded, I could see him waging a war inside himself. He was about to lose it.

Andy took another step closer, so he was only inches away from me. He pulled his hands from his pockets, and rested them on the trunk of my car, one on either side of me. He had me pinned.

"What are you do—" I started to say, and the next thing I knew, his hands were in my hair and his lips were on mine. My mind went completely vacant as I surrendered to him. My lips parted, inviting him in. He slipped his tongue inside my mouth, and his stubble tickled my lips.

My tongue instinctively met his as our kiss began to ignite a fire inside me that Rob had extinguished long ago. Andy moaned quietly as he knotted his fingers firmly in my hair. I pulled him as close as I could get him, and before I knew it, he was reaching down, gripping me behind my knees, and lifting me onto the trunk of my car.

I wrapped my arms around his neck, as he pressed himself between my thighs and slipped his hands up the back of my shirt to touch my bare skin.

Holy hell, I wanted him to yank my clothes off right there!

When he finally broke our heated kiss, he pressed his forehead against mine, but didn't move his body away. We remained attached to one another with our eyes closed, breathing hard and letting our heart rates drop back to normal. His erection pressed against me, and my conscience screamed at me to leave before I changed my mind.

I needed to listen to it.

Without breaking our contact, I reached up and took his face in my hands. I rubbed my thumbs back and forth lightly over his stubbly jaw.

"I need to go," I said quietly and kissed him gently on the lips. He kissed me back, but didn't move.

*"Please,"* I begged, because I needed him to go. After another silent minute, he pulled back and opened his eyes to look at me.

He knotted his fingers in my hair again. "Okay...I already miss you, though," he whispered as he lightly brushed his soft lips across mine. He pushed off my car, turned, and went back up the stairs and into his apartment. He never looked back.

For several minutes, I sat on the trunk of my car, completely paralyzed. One part of me was trying to comprehend what the fuck had just happened, and the other part of me was wondering if I should be chasing him up the stairs to rip off his clothes.

Yep, I needed to get the hell out of there. Quick.

While I sat in my car letting it warm up, I sent him a text.

> *Thank you for the text last night. I listened to the song several times. I get it, and I hear you loud and clear. I'm sorry for everything.*

Before he could respond, I shut off my phone and put it in the glove box.

# Chapter Eighteen

## Christmas Eve 2011

For two weeks, I'd been staying with my mom and dad. I skipped out on work and I started seeing my former therapist. When I left my apartment the day after my birthday, I drove around aimlessly to clear my head, and then made my way to the *only* place where I knew I would feel secure.

I felt a little silly, running home to mommy and daddy, because I had purposely pushed them away. However, I needed to be in the place where I had finally found comfort, safety, and learned how to love and trust all those years ago.

I desperately needed to get my comfort, safety, and trust back. Love was the only thing I had left, and I couldn't lose that too.

When I showed up on their doorstep that afternoon two weeks earlier, they welcomed me in with open arms and minds, as I knew they would. I told them what I needed and how I was ready to get my life back on track.

We talked about the way I was feeling about myself, about Andy, and about what had been going on with Rob.

They knew most of it already, but after the tire incident, and the fact that Rob had gone onto our property to vandalize my car, they were furious.

My dad went to the shop the same day and reviewed all of the security videos. He told me he watched Andy go outside, get in his truck, and leave first thing in the morning. Shortly after that, he saw someone in a black hoody slash my tires and throw the roses all over my car.

Unfortunately, the person's face was never visible, so we knew there was nothing the cops could do about it. My dad fast-forwarded through the video, and a couple hours after Rob had left, Andy came back home with a truckload of bags from shopping.

My dad found nothing else on the video, until right after eleven, when it showed me going out to find my car trashed.

I am sure it showed my kiss with Andy, but if it did, my dad did not mention it. Thank God. However, he did give me kudos for changing my tires all by myself.

The entire first weekend, I sat at my parents' house in my old bedroom, going through my old daily journals, thinking, and listening to music. I called my employees to let them know I would be out until after the New Year and made them promise that if they needed me, they would call me.

The Monday morning after my birthday, I called my former therapist, Dr. Jensen. I made appointments with her for every day she could fit me in through the end of the year, just to begin with. I knew I would continue to see her until I went to Cabo, but that would be a good start. I had health insurance that paid for therapy, so I was going to take advantage of it.

I also felt like a complete idiot because I'd let my life get so out of control that I needed therapy to put it back together.

Dr. Jensen and I discussed, in depth, everything that had happened in my life since I saw her last, which was back in high school. We worked specifically on my guilt over everything Rob did when he sued my father and me. Even though my family tried to tell me it wasn't my fault, I always believed it was.

After my miscarriage, I decided to leave Rob and filed for divorce, but he continued to work at the shop. With the way the laws were, legally, my dad couldn't fire him. The situation was very uncomfortable for everyone involved, but eventually, he quit on his own.

Within two years, I had a miscarriage, divorce, opened a new business, and purchased two apartments. All of this while continuing my job at the shop. I had completely overwhelmed myself.

My life for those two years was like a bad drama movie. I hadn't dealt with it at the time, which in turn, shut me down mentally. Dr. Jensen and I decided I had too many ups and downs all at once. It was like a yo-yo, and similar to me moving between foster homes when I was younger.

It was too unstable for a person like me.

We went back to the way we worked years ago, during my original therapy. We concentrated on me not putting blame on myself for other people's actions, like I had with my birth mom. We worked on me not comparing one situation to another; as in, Andy and Rob were nothing alike. Dr. Jensen said the exact same thing my dad did when I spoke to him about Andy.

She also reminded me that Andy had lost so much in his life too. In all actuality, he was a lot like me.

My birth mom abandoned me willingly for drugs and men. Andy lost his family, tragically. We were both orphans. He had his aunt and uncle, I eventually had the James family. These people took us in with no expectations, and they loved us unconditionally.

Dr. Jensen helped me to believe I needed to treat everything I'd been through in the last few years as learning experiences. The quickest way I was going to get over my issues, was going to be to get out and do things with my friends and family. I needed to let everyone back in, and I needed to talk to them about what I was bottling up inside of me.

If I was going to get anything accomplished, I needed to go cold turkey with the way I was behaving.

While I was at my parents' house, I continued meeting Jess and Sasha for our dance class, and we made a few plans for our trip to Cabo. I was openly talking to my family, and my brothers came by daily to see me. I even took a chance and told them about my feelings for Andy, and that he was the reason I finally realized enough was enough.

Most importantly, I told them I needed to get my life back, and that I was done with being miserable. They were concerned at first, but then the five of us talked about all the things Andy did for me when Rob caused trouble, and how protective he was over me. They admitted how much they liked Andy since they'd come to know him, and they agreed he was worthy of their only sister.

I actually laughed when *they* came to their decision, even though I already decided I was going to try a relationship with him. If he was still willing, that is.

The only thing left for me to do was let Andy in. My nerves were completely shot, yet at the same time, I was excited and ready to see him.

It was Christmas Eve morning, and I woke early and helped my mom with the last few pies we needed to bake for Christmas day. The entire family would be over for the holiday dinner. Because I'd been away for two weeks, I needed to go home, wrap Christmas presents, and bring them back to my parents' house.

My mom mentioned Andy didn't have any plans for Christmas, because his aunt and uncle were going out of town, so I knew he would be home. I hated the fact that he was spending Christmas alone.

After I showered and got ready for the day, I drove home and went straight to Andy's apartment. I knocked twice and held my breath until he answered the door.

"Zoey, you're back," he said, surprised to see me standing outside his door. "Please, come in."

What I really wanted to do right then was jump into his arms and never let him go. Instead, I stayed calm and walked past him to the living room. I shoved my hands inside the pockets of my hoody, so I would keep them to myself for the time being.

Seeing him now, after two weeks, was exactly what I needed to remind me of why I had to get my shit together. I missed him more than I ever thought I would.

Everything about him, his gorgeous blue eyes, his golden skin, the way he smelled, and the way he looked at me—like he wanted to eat me alive—was exhilarating. Nobody ever looked at me the way Andy did. There was always a hint of hunger, excitement, and something else in his eyes.

I desperately wanted to find out what that something else was.

Mostly, I needed to feel the way he made me feel when I was with him. I needed it to sink in and...to just be there. The two weeks without seeing or talking to him had weighed heavily on my conscience. It wasn't fair to him, but I couldn't be what we both needed if I wasn't open and willing to try.

"How are you doing?" I finally asked.

He smiled at me. "Great, now that you're here. I was worried about you. Your mum told me you were doing well when I asked about you."

I was thrilled he had asked her about me. "I've been staying with them," I said. I was so anxious to tell him everything, my body was actually vibrating from the inside out. I also didn't want him to think I was crazy, but I needed him to know what I'd been up to the last two weeks.

"I have a lot to tell you, but I need to do some of it gradually, if it's alright with you," I said cautiously.

He nodded, obviously concerned about me. "Zoey, I want to hear everything you need to say. It's not going to change the way I feel about you."

*Here goes nothing.*

"Sooo...I've been going to therapy," I admitted as I stared down at the old Converse on my feet, a little ashamed by my confession. After I said it, I lifted my head and watched his face to gauge his reaction. He almost seemed nervous, but motioned for me to sit on the couch, and when I did, he sat down next to me.

"Are you okay?" he asked pensively, as if he had no idea how to respond to my disclosure.

In response to his question, I nodded. "Don't worry," I said lightly. "I'm not crazy or anything."

I laughed at what I said, and he looked at me oddly. He missed my private joke. That or I really was crazy. Nothing like making yourself *look* crazy by telling someone you are *not* crazy. I shook the thought from my head and took a deep breath before continuing.

Because I was so nervous, I actually wrote down everything I wanted to tell him first, so I wouldn't forget what was most important. The paper was folded up in my back pocket, just in case I had a hard time getting the words out.

"The last few years have been a little rough, and I didn't deal with my problems when they happened. I put up walls and shut myself inside them. I'm seeing the same therapist I went to after my adoption, and she's been helping me a lot the last two weeks," I explained.

"I think that's great, Zoey," he said, whole-heartedly. "Let me know if there's anything I can do to help."

"Thank you. I still have my ups and downs, but I'm working on it," I admitted. "I hope you can be patient with me. There is a lot I want to tell you, but it can wait until later."

He glanced down at my hands that were resting in my lap as if he wanted to touch me, but he was unsure if it was okay. I took the initiative and held my hand out to him. He took it in his, giving a gentle squeeze, before lacing our fingers together.

"Zoey, I'll do anything for you. Whatever you need, please ask." He spoke so sincerely, it made my insides flutter.

"Thank you, that means a lot to me."

I checked the time on my phone, and it was getting late. I still needed to help my mom with dinner, wrap presents, and to ask Andy to spend Christmas with me and my family. Casually, I snuck a look around his apartment and noticed he didn't have a Christmas tree up, or decorations.

"So, what are your plans for the next two days?"

He laughed and shook his head. "I have no plans whatsoever."

"Will you pack a bag and come back to my mom and dad's house to spend Christmas with my family?" I raised my eyebrow and smiled at him.

He chuckled. "Yes."

That made me laugh. "You say *yes* so easily."

He brought our linked hands to his mouth and brushed his lips across the back of my hand. "You should try it sometime," he said, his blue eyes teasing me.

"Also something I'm working on," I replied honestly. I stood from the couch and pulled him to his feet. "Go get ready and pack your bag, while I go home to wrap presents. Come on over when you're ready."

I hugged him tightly around the waist, my body still shaking. I knew he could feel it, because he hugged me tighter and began rubbing his big hands up and down my back.

"Relax, Zoey," he whispered. "You're gonna be alright."

*God, please let him be right.*

Just as I finished wrapping Alex's last Christmas gift, Andy came into my room, carrying a duffle bag. "I need to pack some more clothes, and then I'll be ready to go," I told him. I pulled some pants out of my dresser drawer and tossed them into a bag. I opened another drawer, and on the top of the stack of clothes was Andy's New

Zealand shirt. The same shirt I took from his laundry basket weeks earlier when I found him sleeping at my place.

I held the shirt out to him. "This belongs to you," I said sheepishly since, technically, I'd stolen it from him.

"How'd you get that?" he asked inquisitively, but he did not reach out to take it from me.

I set it down on my dresser and explained to him how I came to have the shirt.

"Keep it. I'm sure it looks better on you anyway."

"Are you sure you don't want to file a missing shirt report?" I joked. "Call the cops on me for grand theft shirt?"

He laughed, tossed his bag on the floor, and then sat down on my bed. "Yeah, I'm sure. I know where it's at if I need to visit it. Besides, I think it would only be considered petty theft, not grand theft," he joked as he reached out and took my hand in his.

"I've missed you, Zoey," he expressed quietly as he gazed up at me. "I've missed what we had together, even if it was only as friends."

I sat next to him on my bed, knowing it was time to tell him more of what I needed to say...that I didn't want to be his friend. I wanted more.

"I'm sorry for everything I've done to hurt you. I swear it wasn't intentional. I've been so messed up for so long..." I trailed off.

I still had a hard time finding the words and explaining my feelings. At times, it would all come rushing forward at once, to where I literally could not form a solid thought to speak. I wished I wrote this part down, but honestly, I wasn't expecting him to bring up the subject first.

"Take your time," he said in a calm, comforting tone. "I want you to get everything sorted out for yourself. Don't worry about me, because I'm not going anywhere."

He put his arm around my shoulder and pulled me close. I wrapped my arms around his waist. I wanted to tell him how I felt about him, well not all of it, but he needed to know some of it. The rest could come later, when I was ready to take that step.

Telling someone I loved them was a big, *big* deal for me. I knew I wasn't ready to tell him yet, and was glad that I hadn't told him when I realized it on my birthday. It would come, eventually, but I needed to wait. Besides, I didn't even know if he still wanted me.

So there I sat, holding onto him while he rubbed comforting circles on my back, patiently waiting for my mind to calm down. When it finally did, I was able to let out some of those thoughts.

"I've had feelings for you since the day I met you, Andy. Literally, the second I turned around and saw you standing there, I could *feel* it. I didn't know what it was at the time, but there was something there. Then we started talking and spending time together, and it was so easy and natural and...normal. I've never felt anything like that with anyone. I hate to admit it, but you sort of scare me."

I pulled back to make eye contact with him. Something else I was working on, being able to face my fears...to look them directly in the eyes.

He narrowed his eyes at me in confusion. "I scare you?"

I shook my head and chuckled at his misunderstanding. "Yes, but it's not as if I'm afraid of you. I've never had anyone affect me the way you do, so that scares me, but only because it's unfamiliar and well...scary."

I couldn't keep from laughing, but luckily, he understood. "Don't worry, Beautiful. You scare me too," he teased.

I squeezed his knee, and he jumped. *Hmm...I think someone might be ticklish.* "Good. At least we're in this together then," I noted.

He chuckled. "Are we now?"

I looked him in the eyes again and nodded. "Yes."

I fell back on the bed, relieved I was finally able to make it through this first step with him. I needed to take this slow, so I didn't get overwhelmed, but I had missed him so much.

Reaching over, I placed my hand on his back and scratched up and down lightly with my fingertips. I felt him physically stiffen, so I pulled away and rested my arm across my stomach.

"I'm sorry. Did I do something wrong?" I asked.

He laid back on the bed next to me, then rolled to his side to face me, propping himself up on his elbow. "Definitely not," he said, a little self-consciously. What could he possibly have to be self-conscious about?

"Then, what is it?" I asked.

"Have you ever had a spot on your body, where someone might touch you, and it sends chills through you?" he asked unexpectedly.

"Good chills or bad chills?" I asked.

"Good," he said suggestively.

"Um, I'm not really sure," I stated honestly after thinking about it for a minute. "So I'm guessing you like your back being touched?"

"It drives me crazy...in a *good* way," he admitted. The way he enunciated the word *good*, I knew exactly what he meant.

*Noted for future reference!*

"This is definitely a conversation for another day." I let out a nervous breath and laughed to ease my tension.

He agreed. "Yes. This is definitely not a conversation for today."

I rolled onto my side to face him, propping myself up on my elbow. "If you still want to see where things go with us, I'm ready to try," I finally said.

His eyes lit up, and a grin eased across his beautiful face. "Are you sure?"

I gave him a reassuring smile. "I'm positive. I don't want anyone else, but I'll understand if you're hesitant now, after all the stupid shit I've pulled."

I needed him to understand why I changed my mind about him. While I was staying at my parents' house, I found the perfect song to explain my feelings when my brain was too weary to form words to speak. When I found the song, I played it repeatedly and cried for hours, because the lyrics moved me so intensely, emotionally.

"Will you listen to a song for me? I think it will help me explain *me* a little better. I'm still having a hard time trying to clarify some of the thoughts in my head."

"Remember, I said I'd do anything for you, and I meant it. Let's check out this song."

After locating my iPod, I scrolled to the song "The Reason" by the band Hoobastank. I handed him my iPod and my ear buds, but instead of him listening to the song alone, he asked me to listen to it with him.

As the song played, he took my hand in his and brought it to his lips to kiss my fingers. The entire time he listened to the song, he was touching me. He reached over and stroked my cheek with his thumb, gently brushing it back and forth. Andy held my hand and comforted me when my eyes became teary because of how he was looking at me while he listened to the words.

In his expression, I saw glimpses of love, worry, and surprise. But most of all, it was the empathy in his eyes that made me break down crying.

I knew, from the look on his face, that he understood why I needed him to listen to it. When the song was over, he took the ear buds and set them on the bed.

"Zoey, am I *the reason?*"

His voice went from speaking normally to a whisper as he finished the sentence. It was an emotional moment for us both. The way he whispered "the reason," I knew he understood what I was trying to tell him. I nodded and let the tears flow freely, without worrying what he thought of me.

He pulled me into his arms and let me cry. "Let it all go, Beautiful," he whispered as he gently brushed his fingers through my hair.

So many things were going through my mind that I wanted to tell him, and for once, I knew I could. Andy listening to the song with me had brought it all to the surface.

"If I could have played this song for you the day I left, I would have, so you would have understood why I needed to leave. *You* are the reason for everything I've done in the last two weeks. You are the reason we are sitting here now. I was so fucking lost until I met you. My life was on a downward spiral, and I wanted out of it, but there was no reason for me to try."

I took a deep breath as he wiped the tears off my cheeks and let me continue.

"Then, you came here and changed everything. When we danced on my birthday, I was so happy...and I wanted to tell you that I wanted to be with you. When you rejected me, I swear it felt like my entire world dropped out from under me..."

My voice faltered at the memory, and I had to stop to compose myself.

"Andy, I'm so sorry I hurt you that night. When you texted me and asked me to listen to the song after you left...I knew I needed to do something. Your leaving was the best thing you could have done for me. I hope you understand that."

He squeezed me tighter and whispered the most amazing words in my ear. "I do, Zoey. Who else gets you the way I do? It killed me to walk away from you, but I didn't know what else to do to get your attention. You shut me out, and I hated it. I'm sorry if I hurt you, too. Will you forgive me?"

I pulled away from him and held his face in my hands. "There is nothing to forgive. If anything, I need to thank you for making me realize I needed to let go and start over. Thank you...for being *my reason*. Every single word of that song is meant for you. I want to be the perfect person for you, and I am going to try with everything I have if you'll let me."

"I don't want to rush you, Zoey. It hasn't been very long since you left. I'm still worried about you."

Obviously, I understood why he was worried, but I could deal with it. "One day at a time, then?"

"Yes. Can I kiss you now?"

"Yes!" I responded enthusiastically.

"See, it wasn't so hard to say yes, was it?" he teased.

"Well," I said with a hint of sarcasm, "when the question is whether you can *kiss* me or not...there is no way in hell I'm saying no."

I'd been waiting since I woke up that morning for that very second. I leaned forward and met his lips with mine. His lips parted, and I eased my tongue inside his mouth, meeting his. He was letting me control the situation, and I appreciated it more than he would ever know.

We continued to kiss, but I didn't want to go overboard, so I slowly pulled back and rested my forehead on his. Merely stopping everything, and resting against each other like that, took all the bad feelings and nervousness away.

When he had pressed his forehead to mine two weeks earlier, when I was leaving, it was the most calming, peaceful feeling I'd experienced in ages. Aside from it being insanely hot too, that is.

"We better get going before everybody wonders where we're at."

He pressed his lips to mine one last time before we loaded our bags and Christmas packages into my Audi and headed over to my parents' house.

# Chapter Nineteen

We arrived at my parents' and packed our first armload of presents inside. It took two trips to get everything out of my car. After we put all the presents around the base of the tree, my two nephews ambushed us.

"Aunt Zoey!" Jake yelled, as Alex ran to me holding up his arms so I would pick him up.

I knelt down on the floor, and they both slammed into me for a hug. I picked them up, one in each arm, and headed to the living room with them giggling. I playfully tossed them onto the couch and introduced them to Andy. Alex was a bit shy, so he didn't say much. Jake, on the other hand, he was a talker.

Andy knelt down in front of them on the floor. "Eh, guys," he said, way over exaggerating his accent. "Are you two ready to open all those Chrissy pressies over there tomorrow morning?" He pointed to all their presents under the tree. Both boys stared at him with surprised expressions on their faces.

"Anny talks funny, Aunt Zoey," Jake squealed. Everyone laughed, including Andy. Little Jake had a hard time saying his D's, so we were amused at him calling Andy, Anny.

My sister-in-law, Heather, scolded her son. "Jake, it's not nice to say that someone talks funny." She didn't even need to tell him to, but Jake apologized to Andy. He knew he'd forgotten his manners. He was such a good kid.

"Andy has an accent that makes him sound different than us," I explained to my nephew. "You know how Grandma sounds when she speaks Spanish, right? It's because she is from Mexico. Andy's from a country called New Zealand, Jakey, so he talks like people from New Zealand."

"Oh, Anny, okay," he said brightly, obviously comprehending what I told him.

Jake jumped off the couch and ran over to the globe my parents kept on a shelf. "Anny, you show me Noo Zeelan?" He smacked the globe with the palm of his hand, sending it spinning on its axis.

"Sure thing, mate," Andy replied happily. He went over to Jake, who had taken the globe from the shelf and sat down on the floor with it.

"Anny, please sit!" Jake demanded excitedly.

Andy covered his mouth to stifle his laugh, as my family watched on amused. He sat next to where Jake was in the middle of the floor. Jake crawled right onto Andy's lap, pulling the globe with him. Andy looked up at me from the floor and grinned.

I swore I felt my ovaries ache when that man smiled up at me. I chuckled at the thought. "I'm going to help Mom. Have fun, you two."

"Mom, we're here," I said when I found her shredding meat for the tamales we were having for Christmas Eve dinner.

"Andy came with you, Mija?" she asked happily.

"Yeah, he did," I replied as I washed my hands at the kitchen sink.

She smiled at me and continued working. I mixed the masa for the tamales, and then started on the salsa. Jess and Noah came in just as we were finishing up to see if we needed any help.

"Hey, you made it." I was glad to see Jess, so I could tell her about Andy.

"Sorry we're late, but we needed to stop at the store. I made a cheesecake, and you-know-who refuses to eat it without whipped cream. Even though we all know it totally ruins cheesecake," she joked as she playfully elbowed my brother in the ribs.

Noah gave me a one armed hug around the shoulders. "Hi, sis, it's good to see you *both* here."

I hugged him back. "Thanks. I'm glad he came."

Noah kissed me on the side of the head and left the kitchen after a mischievous swat to Jess's butt.

"So, Zoey," Jess said inquisitively. "You and Andy are together now, huh?"

It took less than two minutes for the inquisition to begin.

I smiled nervously. "We're going to give it a try, day by day."

She hugged me. I mean, she *really* hugged me. Not a quick meaningless hug, but the kind of hug you get from someone who truly loves you and is happy for you. I hugged her back the same way.

"I'm so happy for you, Z." She held me at arm's length, looking me in the eyes. "Noah really likes him, and the first time I see him, he's sitting on the floor with a four-year-old. That says a lot about him."

I nodded, tears suddenly stinging my eyes. "Jess, I'm scared to death."

Jess pulled me back into a hug. "You love him, don't you?" she whispered.

She knew me too well. I mumbled something resembling the word yes.

"It's a good thing, Z. You deserve to be happy. You know that, right?"

Before I answered, I heard a noise and looked up as Andy pushed open the kitchen door. He paused when he saw me, trying to decide if he should come in or not. I let go of Jess.

"Hey, come in. We're just having a moment." I smiled to reassure him. "Did you two meet yet?" They both said yes at the same time, and then made small talk while I wiped away the tears that spilled over when I blinked.

"Jessie, can you help me set the table?" my mom called from the dining room. Jess grinned and left the room to help my mom. It would be another hour before we ate, so I knew my mom was giving me a minute alone with Andy.

"Sorry," he said. "I came in to get a juice box for Jake. I didn't mean to interrupt you and Jess. Are you alright?"

He stayed where he was as he waited for my answer. Taking the initiative, I went to him instead. "Yeah, I'm good. I promise. Jess and I were talking about you," I admitted.

"And it made you cry?" he asked seriously.

"Don't worry. It was a *good* cry."

He slipped his arms around me and leaned back against the counter, pulling me with him. We stood in silence, his chin resting on the top of my head. I loved that we didn't need to say anything to feel the connection with each other. It was just there.

"What are you lovely ladies making in here?" he asked after a few minutes. "It smells delicious." We still held on to each other as I told him what we were having for dinner.

The kitchen door swung open and Jake ran in. "Anny!" he called, "I lost Noo Zeelan!"

We pulled away from each other. "I'll help you find it again, mate," Andy told him as he hoisted Jake up over his shoulder and took him to the fridge for his juice.

"I better get back to work on this food if we want to eat sometime today," I said. Andy reached over and stroked my cheek with his free hand. Silent words of understanding passed between us.

I grinned at Andy because he was so at ease with my nephew. Darn my aching ovaries, they were making me think crazy things.

"Bye, Aunt Zoey!" Jake yelled as they turned and left the room.

When dinner was ready, we sat around the long dining room table and passed around platters of food, filling our plates. It was nice to be with my entire family and Andy. He really did fit in well with all of us. He joked around with my brothers, played with my nephews, and helped clean up after dinner.

The guys played several rounds of poker, as the girls sat and talked, and the kids took much needed naps. I caught up on what was going on in the lives of my sister-in-law, Heather, and Adam's girlfriend, Angie. It had been too long since I'd seen them.

I also wished Jeremy would find a decent woman soon. He was going to be single forever if he didn't get his shit together. I worried about him the most. He was an awesome person, but really needed a woman who would calm him down some. At age twenty-eight, he was enjoying the single life and had girls fawning over him wherever he went. He had gorgeous olive-colored skin and dark hair like my mom, and was tall and fit like my dad. He also inherited my dad's big blue-gray eyes and long, thick eyelashes. I had heard many times, from all my girlfriends, it was a lethal combination.

We gathered back in the dining room for Jess's cheesecake and some frosted Christmas cookies that Heather had made. Jason stood up from his seat at the table as we were eating.

"Heather and I have an announcement," he said proudly.

Everyone went completely silent, waiting for it, even though we already knew what he was going to say. We'd heard the same speech twice before.

"Well, get on with it already," my dad teased as he beamed up at his first-born son.

"We're gonna have another baby," Jason said excitedly.

Heather stood and kissed him on the cheek, and he placed his hand on her still flat stomach.

"We found out a while ago, but we wanted to wait until everyone was together to announce it. I'm due at the beginning of July," Heather added.

She was already glowing. My sister-in-law was a wonderful mom, and I hoped I would be like her someday.

The room filled with happy chatter and questions about whether they wanted a boy or a girl this time.

I stood and hugged my brother and his wife. "I'm happy for you two. Congratulations." The family took turns congratulating them, while I sat on my chair and pushed my slice of cheesecake around on my plate.

My mind started racing with thoughts of the future; *my* possible future, if this relationship worked out with Andy. He was good with my nephews and seemed to like kids. We were both married before, and I had been pregnant. Would he want to get married again and have kids?

*One day at a time, Zoey. One day at a time!*

I calmed myself back down, but Andy had already noticed my tension. He squeezed my hand, and his eyebrows furrowed, as a silent question passed between us. I squeezed his hand back, letting him know I was okay.

Later that night, everyone said their goodbyes and headed to their homes. We told my mom and dad goodnight, and then went into my bedroom. Andy kicked off his shoes and laid face down on the bed, complaining because he ate too much, but couldn't stop himself from doing it, because everything tasted so good.

I'd had several thoughts swimming around in my head for the past few hours, most of them revolving around marriage and kids. "Andy? You're going to be a great dad someday," I blurted out as I unpacked the bag I brought from home.

He raised up on his elbows and looked over at me with a startled expression on his face. "Where did *that* come from, Zoey?"

I giggled at his question. "You were good with my nephews today. Jake absolutely loved you," I noted. "Even if he did call you Anny."

He chuckled. "He's a good kid. Very inquisitive."

I finished unpacking my clothes and tossed the empty bag into the closet. "Andy?" I wasn't sure how to bring up the subject, so I spilled everything. "I'm on the pill, just so you know. And I've had all the other tests done for STDs too, so if the time comes, we don't need to worry about that." I laid down on the bed next to him and scooted close, facing him.

"Zoey that conversation can wait for another day too."

"No, it's fine. I want to talk about it. I think we should talk about as much as we can and get to know each other better. Is that okay with you?"

"Of course," he replied. "I'll do anything you need me to."

I felt a little guilty, putting all of my issues on him, but he needed to know me. I got an idea, so I gathered the family photo albums and brought them back to my room. We sat on the bed and went through them together. He thought it was sad that there were no photos of me prior to age fourteen.

"I don't even know what I looked like as a baby," I said sadly. "Almost everything in my life before I came here is a blur."

Andy slowly flipped through the pages, taking in everything. He stopped when he found several photos of me from high school. "What were you like in school?" he asked.

I sighed, knowing I wanted to tell him about my past, but dreaded telling him. He needed to understand the reasons why I was the way I was.

"I wasn't the greatest teenager," I admitted. "I got decent grades, and did well in choir, but for the first two years of high school, I was angry and...oh God." I paused. This was harder than I thought. Was he going to think less of me, because of the stupid shit I did, because nobody taught me right from wrong growing up?

He reached over and laced his fingers with mine. "Take your time. We don't have to rush this."

I knew that, but I wanted to be done with it, so I continued. "Not having grown up with a male role model and with my birth mom being the way she was with men, I thought that's how I was supposed to act with boys...so I sort of acted out a bit...um, sexually."

He studied me, and I could see the distress in his eyes. "I'm sorry, Zoey," he said. "I had no idea."

I knew he would have questions, so I told him my story. "I lost my virginity two months after I started high school. I was at a party where I wasn't supposed to be. It was a dumb thing to do."

His fingers tightened around mine, comforting me. I took a breath and continued. "To make a long story short, I was sad, angry, and rebellious for the next two years, so I slept with a few more guys...I let them use me, because I really didn't care about myself. Somehow, my mom found out, and she stuck me in therapy."

Letting out a long sigh, he shut the photo album and set it on the bed.

"Have I told you too much, too soon?" I asked. "I don't want to scare you away."

He shook his head. "No, I told you I'm not going anywhere. I had no idea you'd been through so much. I didn't think about how you grew up, and how it would affect you later on in life." He sat for a minute, staring at me. I could tell he was uneasy with the information I had disclosed.

Regardless, I needed to finish the story, so I started talking again. "I went to therapy and stopped acting out like that. I didn't need to do it, because I learned it wasn't how 'normal' people were supposed to act and treat each other. I met Rob my senior year, went to college, got married, things happened, and we divorced."

After taking a breath, I continued. "I actually dated someone for a few months after we separated, but it obviously didn't work out. I always had a suspicion Rob somehow ran him off, but I didn't try to find out."

I stopped talking, so Andy would have time to absorb everything I told him. We sat in silence for an eternity. "Andy, say something," I begged and scooted closer to him.

"I feel like an asshole," he finally said.

*Huh?* "Why would you say that?" I asked, confused.

"Because, Zoey, prior to the accident, I lived an extremely charmed life. I always had everything I ever wanted. I feel now, like I took it for granted. My issues were nothing compared to what you've gone through. I was one of those guys in school who had sex with girls because I could. I never thought about how they felt or how I treated them."

I was surprised at what he was saying. He didn't seem like the type of person to do that. "Were you popular in school?" I asked.

He smirked guiltily. "Yeah, you could say so." He looked at me with shame in his eyes. "I was the star rugby player, rich kid, had girls all over me all the time, and took what I wanted from them and let them go."

"Well," I retorted, "aren't we a pair?" I stole his line from the first time we ate dinner together the day we met.

He frowned. "After the accident, I didn't go back to school. I quit playing rugby, got into some trouble, and then we moved to the US. I started all over here, and I quit being a dick to girls."

He had a tough time after his family died, and I felt bad for him. At least nobody died on me. They just ditched me.

"Now you're not a dick," I stated to reassure him. "You're a good man, Andy."

He leaned over and kissed me on the side of the head. "Thank you, Zoey. That means a lot coming from you."

It had been a long day. I was exhausted, and he looked like he was too. "I think we should get some sleep. I'm tired, and you look like you could use some sleep too."

"Yeah, you're right. Where am I sleeping?"

"With me, of course," I said, patting my bed. "But, no funny business, okay?"

"Are you sure I should be staying in here with you? Are your parents alright with it?"

"I don't want you to stay anywhere else. They're as happy to have you here as I am."

He smiled, and we both got ready for bed. He came back from the bathroom wearing a pair of black flannel pajama shorts and slipped into bed next to me. We each turned off our lamps.

"Goodnight, Sexy," I mumbled as he nestled up behind me and slid his arm around me.

He chuckled and kissed my bare shoulder. "Goodnight, Beautiful."

# Chapter Twenty

The day after Christmas, I took Andy home and then went back to my mom and dad's. I wanted him to stay a while longer, but I knew I needed to take my time and ease in to a relationship with him. I didn't want too much, too soon. He agreed it was a good idea.

Originally, I planned to stay with my parents until after New Year's, and I was doing fairly well since starting therapy with Dr. Jensen. It was nice to talk to someone who was unbiased and truly wanted to help me without his or her own agenda. After sitting down and talking to Andy, I hoped everything would start falling into place for us.

On New Year's Eve, Will called to remind me that he and Justin were throwing their annual New Year's party at their place and that my attendance was required. It sounded like fun, and I would get to visit all of my old friends that I'd lost contact with.

Deciding to go to the party, I packed my bags to return home for good on New Year's Eve. I wanted to start the new year off right. I was looking forward to starting a new year and a new lease on life. I needed it, and I wanted it. I was trying hard to stay optimistic, but I'd been feeling a little bit down that day, so I thought the party would help cheer me up.

When I turned the corner next to my apartment, I was glad I had private parking over at the shop parking lot. The entire street was lined with cars. It looked like they were having a big party this year. Normally, the party wasn't quite so large.

Anxious to see Andy, I didn't feel like packing my bags back to my apartment right then, so I took only my purse, leaving everything else in my trunk. I let myself into the lobby and began walking up the stairs.

People were milling around the lobby and stairs, drinking and having a good time. The boys had set out several extra chairs in the lobby, so people wouldn't be so cramped inside their apartment. I heard the music playing through the open door upstairs.

At the first landing, I made a left to the second smaller set of stairs that led to the landing in front of our doors. Andy was leaning against the wall outside my door, a beer in his hand, and talking to two girls. I was unable to hear what the girls were saying, but they seemed very intrigued with what *he* was saying.

A little pang of jealousy went through me, so I stopped on the stairs and watched them for a minute. Part of my therapy was learning how I shouldn't jump to conclusions, so the situation was a great test for me.

Andy's body language told me he was not being flirty at all, which eased my mind. He was talking loud enough, so I caught a few words he was saying. He was talking about New Zealand.

As I started up the steps again, Andy stopped talking mid-sentence and glanced in my direction. It was almost as if he *knew* I was there. He excused himself from the girls, and in two long strides, was standing in front of me.

"Zoey!" He enveloped me in his arms and picked me up in a bear hug. I flung my arms around him, and he stood holding me in the air, my feet dangling off the ground. He tipped his head back and kissed me in front of everyone. I'd say he was happy to see me.

He set me back down after another quick peck on the lips. "Are you here for the party?"

I shook my head and smiled.

"Are you home to stay, then?"

"Yes."

He looked around behind me. "Where's your luggage?"

I found my apartment keys, took his hand in mine, and went to my door. "It's in my car. I'll get it tomorrow. I wanted to see you first."

I unlocked my door, pulled him inside, and shut it in the faces of the two girls he'd been talking to when I arrived.

We went to the kitchen where I poured myself a glass of Moscato and hopped onto the countertop to sit. "Were you having a good time at the party? We can go back out there if you want to." I took a sip of my wine and waited for his answer.

"It was okay, until you showed up." He set his beer down and stepped forward, so that he was standing between my knees. "Now it's perfect."

I pulled him even closer. "I'm glad to hear you say that. I was kinda worried when I came up the stairs and found you with not one, but two girls hanging on your every word."

He narrowed his blue eyes at me, but when I smiled at him, he realized I was messing with him. "Did you get jealous?"

I shrugged and turned away from him. "Maybe a little at first."

Andy gently pulled my chin back so I had to look at him. He smiled and placed his palms on the countertop on either side of me. "Just so you know, when those girls started talking to me, I was heading over here where it's quieter, to call you."

He moved even closer and slid his hands up my arms, across my shoulders, up the sides of my neck, and into my hair. He left my skin warm and tingling in all the places he touched. His eyes burned into mine, as he slowly wet his gorgeous lips with his tongue.

"I was going to tell you how much I missed you," he whispered and lightly touched my lips with his own.

*Holy hell.*

He closed his eyes as he tangled his fingers tighter in my hair and pressed his forehead to mine. "I was going to tell you how beautiful you are."

He trailed kisses across my cheek. "I was going to tell you how much I need you."

With his warm breath in my ear he whispered, "I was going to tell you how much I want you."

He nipped my ear and began kissing his way back toward my lips. "I was going to tell you how smart, funny, amazing, and strong you are."

By the time his lips met mine, I was completely out of my mind wanting him. I wanted to rip his clothes off right there in my kitchen.

He gripped my hips, slowly pulling me closer to him. I was now at the edge of the counter, so I swung my legs around his hips and locked my ankles together. I wrapped my arms around his neck, deepening our kiss. He moaned as he swept his warm, moist tongue into my mouth and brushed it against mine, repeatedly. His stubble was slightly prickly on my lips and face.

I had kissed him a few times before, but his facial hair was still a very new sensation for me. I'd only ever kissed men who shaved regularly. It was surprisingly erotic to me; somewhat ticklish, yet very masculine, and extremely sexy. It was not at all what I expected, but I loved it.

Releasing my arms from around his neck, I ran my hands down his chest. He loosened his grip from my hips as my hands traveled further down his abs and then up under his shirt to touch his hot skin. Holy fuck, I needed to stop this before it went too far. I ended the kiss, and a small moan emanated from my throat when our lips broke contact. I didn't pull back all the way, but rested my forehead against his, trying to catch my breath, my hands still under his shirt, gripping his sides.

I stopped my hands there, because I knew if I let them wander around to his back where I really wanted them to go, it might get me in some trouble. I hadn't forgotten his admission to me about his back being his erogenous zone.

He reached up, stroked my cheek with his fingertips, and brushed my hair behind my ear.

"You know, Sexy," I whispered breathlessly, my forehead still resting against his. "You make it awfully difficult for a girl who is trying really, *really* hard to say yes more often, to tell herself no right now."

He let out a deep chuckle. "Is that so?"

"Yes!"

He laughed and took a step away from me. I pushed myself backward onto the countertop and looked at him. "You need to take me to the party before I change my mind," I joked.

He helped me down off the counter, took my hand in his, and led me next door to the party. Darn, I was hoping he would turn toward my bedroom instead of the front door. I needed to give myself a little shove in that direction when the time came. *Wait, Zoey. It will be worth it.*

We were obviously extremely attracted to each other, and after what happened in the kitchen, and everything he said to me, I was sure I wasn't making a mistake wanting to be with him. I knew we would be good together.

When we arrived at the party, he made me feel like I was the only one in the room. He was attentive, affectionate, and he treated me like a queen. It was completely opposite of everything I had ever known in my previous relationships.

Rob and I went to parties while we were together, but as soon as we walked through the door, he ditched me for his friends and drinking games.

Andy introduced me to people he met at the party before I arrived. When he did, he introduced me as "my girl, Zoey," and I loved it. I wanted to be his, and for him to be mine. Not in a possessive, creepy way, but I wanted it to be in a way where there were no questions about us being with each other, exclusively.

We took turns all night getting each other drinks. I introduced him to my friends, and he finally met Sasha. She was as mesmerized by him as I was. Andy went to get us another beer, leaving Sasha and me alone to talk.

"Zoey," she said after Andy was out of earshot. "That man is so in love with you, it's not even funny."

Even though I was unsure if Sasha was right, I smiled. "Hopefully you're right, because I feel the exact same way about him."

We sat down on the couch, and Sasha struck up a conversation with the person on the other side of her. I people watched for a while and wondered where Andy had gotten off to, since he was only getting beer refills. I finally spotted him over by the doorway with an armload of beer bottles.

He seemed uninterested in the person who was talking to him. It was one of the girls from the landing.

Ugh. I hadn't seen her in a few years, but it finally dawned on me who it was. She had dyed her naturally blonde hair a dark shade of brown, so I didn't recognize her when she was talking to Andy outside my door. Her name was Nicole, and I hated her.

She'd been with Jeremy and most of his friends. I thought she'd been with Rob, too, but of course, I could never prove it. I needed to rescue Andy, before she tried to sink her claws into him the way she did with every other guy within reach.

Halfway to him, everyone started yelling the countdown for midnight and crowded in around me. *Shit!* I knew it was cheesy, but I wanted to kiss him at midnight to start our new year together off right. I pushed my way through the crowd, and as I did, I kept my eyes on Andy and Nicole. He turned around, his eyes searching for me.

The countdown was at five, so I pushed harder through the crowd. He saw me trying to get to him, and he began pushing through to get to me. Right as everyone yelled "Happy New Year," we met in the crowd. He still had an armload of beer bottles, but my hands were free. I helped him set the beers down on the table, as everyone around us kissed whomever they were standing with at that moment.

"I thought you were going to get stuck kissing Nicole for a minute there, Sexy," I teased.

Andy smirked and shook his head. "No way, I'm all yours. These lips won't kiss anyone but you." He gently cupped my face and bent down to kiss me. The second our lips met, everyone else in the room disappeared from my thoughts. He pulled back from our kiss and said, "Happy New Year, beautiful Zoey."

"Happy New Year to you, too. Let's get out of here so we can be alone. It's been too long since I've seen you." I pulled him down and kissed him again. We told our friends goodbye and went back over to my place.

"Stay here tonight?" I asked him as we walked through my door.

"Are you sure?"

"Yeah, let's go watch a movie in my bedroom, since there's still a party going on over there." We picked a few comedies from my DVD collection and took them to my bedroom.

Realizing all my bathroom necessities were still in my car, I hunted through the cabinets and found my supply of new toothbrushes. I had the habit of using a new one every month, so I bought them in bulk. Yet another thing that followed me from foster care, since I had been forced to share toothbrushes, too, on several occasions.

I brushed my teeth and got ready for bed. I wanted Andy to feel comfortable with me and be comfortable at my place, so I left a toothbrush out for him, too. When I went back into my bedroom, I found him still dressed, sitting on the edge of my bed.

"Hey, I left a toothbrush in there for you."

He stood and walked over to me. "Thank you." He kissed me on the cheek, went into the bathroom, and shut the door.

While he was getting ready for bed, I turned down the covers, stacked as many pillows as I could find against the headboard, and set up the movie to watch. The music was still thumping next door, and I knew we would be awake for a while. It was chilly, so I slipped into bed to wait for him.

When Andy came out, I was propped against the pillows watching the New Year's party in New York. He was wearing only gray boxer briefs that left *nothing* to the imagination, and he looked sexy as hell in them.

*"Jesus, are you trying to kill me?"* I muttered under my breath as he walked past the foot of the bed.

He glanced over his tattooed shoulder at me as he stacked his folded clothes on top of my dresser. "Did you say something?"

I shook my head, embarrassed that he heard me.

The lights were still on in my bedroom, so I had a full view of his entire body. He was breathtaking with his naturally golden skin. He was muscular, athletic, long, and lean. Beautifully tattooed. Sinewy. Male. Sexy.

Good God, I wanted to kiss and lick every inch of him. Someday soon, I hoped I would. I learned many little tricks from the blowjob conversation I had with Justin, and I really wanted to try them out.

I watched him as he walked across the room to shut off the lights and as he made his way back to my bed.

He sat down on the bed with his feet still on the floor. "Zoey, are you still sure about this?" he asked.

"What do you mean?" I was a little confused about what he was asking.

"Are you sure you've given yourself enough time?" he clarified.

Ah, yes. He wanted to know if I was going to freak out and push him away. I hurt him before, and I would never do it again. I knew he was what I wanted, and I was not going to fuck up twice.

"I'm saying *yes*, Andy. I still need time to deal with some of my issues. All I am asking for is patience. Please don't give up on me." He was staring at me as if he was trying to figure out if I was being sincere.

When I couldn't stand the silence any longer, I sat up and looked him the eyes. "Please say something. You're making me nervous." He let out a long sigh as he rested back against the pillows and slipped under the covers with me.

He still hadn't said anything, so I spoke up, "I know we've talked about it before, and we agreed to take it one day at a time. I still want that, and I still want you. Please tell me I'm not too late. Did I ruin everything?"

He stayed quiet for another minute as he took in everything I told him. "As long as you're still sure," he finally said. "You know what I want. Besides, would I be here in your bed if it was too late?"

I scooted closer to him and slid my hand across his stomach to rest it on his hip, right at the edge of his boxer briefs. "I guess not...but if you're gonna be staying here overnight again, we're gonna have to work on your bedroom attire. I'm not sure how much longer I can stand seeing you wearing these sexy things," I teased as I ran my fingertips under his waistband and across his stomach. He shivered at my boldness.

*Shit...I even shivered at my boldness.*

I didn't know where my nerve came from to be so assertive with him just then. I had officially shocked myself. This man drew out emotions that I didn't know were inside me. Kissing him was one thing, but sticking my fingertips in the front of his underwear...yeah, that was another story.

He propped himself up on his elbow and got a devious gleam in his eyes as he leaned toward me. "If you don't like my *attire*," he said playfully, "next time you can stay at my place. I don't wear *anything* to sleep, so you won't have to look at them then." He chuckled and flopped back against the pillows again.

*Holy fucking shit.*

"I'll have to remember that," I replied, definitely needing to get my mind off *that* mental picture. "Movie time!" I said abruptly and pressed play on the remote.

We laid there for a while watching the movie together. When a beach scene came on, it reminded me I was going to be in Cabo at the end of the month. I hadn't told Andy yet, so I paused the movie and looked at him apprehensively.

"What's up, Zoey?" he asked as he snuggled in closer to me.

"I need to tell you about my vacation."

"What vacation?"

I hoped he wouldn't be too upset, since I was throwing a big fat wrench into our new relationship.

"I'm going to stay in Mexico for a month with my aunt and uncle. I'm so sorry I forgot to mention it with everything else that's been going on. It's been planned for a few months." I felt terrible for forgetting to tell him.

"You're leaving for a month?" he asked, taken aback. "How are we going to do this if you're gone?"

I thought about it briefly, because I wasn't entirely sure how to respond. "I guess we spend as much time together as we can before I leave. Then, while I'm gone, we can call and text each other. Do you have a computer? We can video chat on Skype. You can wear your sexy bedroom attire, too, so I don't miss them."

I laughed, but he did not.

"I don't have a computer, Zoey," he admitted as he scooted even closer to me, his head now on my pillow. "Looks like I'll be getting one now, though."

"Sounds like a good plan," I said as I nestled into him, sliding my arm across his chest. I closed my eyes and drifted off.

Waking up the next morning after the best sleep I'd had in more than two years, I found myself still wrapped in the arms of the most incredible man I'd ever known. For the first time in my life, I was content.

# Chapter Twenty-One

A week later, it was clear that Andy and I were completely absorbed in one another. We spent every spare second together, really getting to know each other. We ate dinner together every night, and we frequently stayed the night with each other.

I actually slept better when he was with me. Most nights, no dreams or nightmares invaded my sleep. My mind rarely woke me nightly to stare at the walls and ceiling. I don't know if it was because I felt safe with him there, or if it was simply because I was looking forward to my life and was finally relaxed enough to enjoy it, instead of living in the past.

On Thursday night of an extremely busy workweek, I had dance class again. I was working at the store most of the week because one of our employees, Jerry, came down with a horrible case of the flu.

I was hardly spending time with Andy, except for a few minutes when he came next door to the store to pick up a case of oil. I saw him every night, but during the day, I couldn't just stand up from my desk if I wanted to see him, since I was working at the store.

Arriving at class a few minutes early, I sat in my car and sent him a quick text.

*Made it to class. Feels like I haven't seen you in days. I miss you.*

It was amazing how the last weeks since Christmas had changed for us. I received a reply back from him while I was walking through the entrance of the dance studio.

*Stay with me tonight? I promise to be wearing the proper bedroom attire.*

His response made me laugh out loud as I typed out *"yes"* and hit send.

Once I made it home from class, I showered and dressed in my pajamas, some fuzzy slippers, and a jacket. I grabbed my keys and locked up my place, then jogged across the courtyard, because it was freezing outside and my hair was still damp.

Running up the stairs to Andy's apartment door, I considered knocking, but wasn't sure if he was asleep already, or if he was awake waiting for me. I decided to use my keys to let myself in, so I wouldn't wake him if he were sleeping.

His apartment was dark inside, but I had lived there before, so I easily found my way in the dark. I went to his bedroom, and he was asleep. I slipped my cold body under the covers, sliding right up next to him to get warm. I ran my hand down from his hip to his knee. He was wearing a pair of pajama shorts. *Darn.*

"Are you happy with my bedroom attire?" he asked, sounding half-asleep.

I laughed softly. "No, not really, but I guess I'll have to live with it."

Andy rolled over to face me. "I've missed you." He pulled me closer and kissed me. He must have had a long day, too. He sounded as tired as I felt.

"Goodnight," I murmured against his lips. I draped my arm over him and settled against his bare chest, instantly wrapped within his warmth. He immediately fell back to sleep. I'd been hoping to fool around a bit, but I decided to let him sleep. Things had gotten a little hot and heavy with us the last week, and it was taking its toll on me. I'd gone too long without sex or a man's touch.

When I woke the next morning, he was gone. I was in his bed, so I was sure he hadn't gone far. His bedside clock said it was just after six. As I rubbed my eyes, I heard the shower turn on in the bathroom across the hall.

Creeping out of bed, I tiptoed into the bathroom and combed my fingers through my hair. I picked up his mouthwash from the counter and gargled a bit of it, since my toothbrush was at home. I gathered up my nerve, and stripped off my pajamas, letting them fall to the bathroom floor.

I was ready to take another big step with him. Not sex yet, but I needed him...in other ways. With a shaking hand, I slid the shower curtain back quietly and stepped in behind him. I was so nervous, my breathing quickened and the butterflies in my stomach took flight at the sight of him.

He was even more magnificent standing there completely bare. Water and soap cascaded down his muscular tattooed back, gorgeous ass, and legs. *Jesus, how does a man get an ass like that?* It was round, yet muscular and firm looking.

He was washing his face, so I wrapped my arms around his waist and rested my cheek on his back to steady myself. My body would not stop shaking. "You know, I don't like waking up in an empty bed," I said quietly.

It felt like I startled him. He rinsed his face and turned to me, wiping the water from his eyelids. "What do you think you're doing in here?" he asked as he smiled down at me. He wrapped his arms around me, dripping soap and water down my sides and back.

When the water hit my body, I noticed it was almost cold. *Ah, he needed a cold shower.* Poor Andy. I knew all too well how he felt, though. I felt like I needed a few myself recently.

"I thought this would be a good way to spend a little more time with you, since we've both been so busy," I admitted shyly.

Since the water was too cool for me, I reached past him and turned it up to hot. I carefully stepped around him to stand under the showerhead. He stood and watched me as I wet my hair and body. When I was completely soaked, I squeezed some of his bottled soap on a net shower sponge and started washing my body.

He watched me a bit longer, intrigued, his eyes wandering brazenly over my body. He did not make me feel self-conscious in the least.

"You're going to smell like a man all day now, Zoey," he smirked.

I didn't mind. "Yes, but I'll smell like my man...and I like the way you smell," I stated a little suggestively.

I peeked at his body, and he was growing hard as I washed myself with his soap and sponge. He didn't try to hide it. *So much for the cold shower he was trying to take.* I held the sponge under the water, rewetting it, and then added more soap.

"Turn around."

Without question, he turned around slowly to face the other direction. I washed down his back, his very firm muscular ass, and kneeled down on the tub floor to wash his legs and feet. *Yep, that is a nice ass.*

I dropped the sponge and used my hands to wash him, skin to skin. His body was incredible. Solid muscles, golden skin, and a light layer of dark blond hair covered his legs.

Still kneeling on the bathtub floor, I reached up to his hips and urged him to turn and face me. I washed the front of his legs and worked my way up. A narrow trail of hair ran from below his belly button to the most beautiful member of manhood I had ever seen in my life.

No joke. He was freaking perfect. He was also rock hard.

His erection was directly in front of my face, and I couldn't help myself. I had wanted to touch him for days, and now was my chance. I *needed* to touch him. Encircling my trembling fingers around him, I began stroking him with my wet, soapy hand.

"Mmm, Zoey, that feels so good," he whispered.

He gasped as he twitched in my hand, and his hips bucked slightly. I glanced up at him and he was watching me, his eyes already glazed over with desire. I wanted to taste him, so I rinsed the soap from my hand, and then rinsed him off. I wrapped my hand around him again, and took his gorgeous cock into my mouth. Never having done that before, I hoped I was doing it right and that he liked it.

For several minutes, I sucked, licked, and stroked him while he wound his fingers in my hair and caressed my face delicately with his thumbs. His breathing was coming heavier and faster, and I knew he was getting close.

"Zoey, I'm gonna come," he warned moments later.

Not stopping, I continued what I was doing and stared up at him. I wondered if he was expecting me to stop, which I had no intentions of doing. His face was tilted down, his eyes were open and watching me. It was definitely the most erotic moment of my life so far.

His eyes fluttered closed as his body shuddered, and he moaned my name softly as he came. When he was finished, I swallowed and gently released him.

I loved the way he watched me, the way he tenderly touched my face while I pleasured him, and the way he let me finish him off the way *I* wanted to. I wanted every ounce of him inside me, physically and mentally. I knew I would never get enough of him.

My legs shook as I slowly stood. I kissed and licked from his hipbone to his chest, where I flicked my tongue across his nipple. He sucked in a sharp breath, his eyes lingering on mine. I backed under the shower again and pulled him with me. We were both still soapy, and it was beginning to dry on our skin.

Not forgetting I was supposed to be washing him, I slowly rubbed the soapy sponge over his chiseled abs and chest to finish what I'd originally started.

We never took our eyes off each other. "You're amazing, you know that?" he questioned.

Lowering his head, he kissed along my jawline, down my neck and chest to my hardened nipple. He flicked his tongue over it and sucked as he moaned softly. It sent the most breathtaking vibrations through my entire body, and I loved the little noises he made.

Gripping my hips, he turned me, pinning me against the shower wall. Andy began kissing me, his tongue caressing my lips and tongue, his teeth lightly nipping me every so often. He was an amazing kisser, and it had been so long since a man touched me, I could have had an orgasm from only that. His hand eased down my hip and thigh, grasping my leg behind the knee. He slowly lifted it up to rest my foot on the edge of the tub. His hand slid back up my thigh, sliding leisurely over to stroke me with his long, broad fingers.

I was wet and ready, and already on the verge of orgasm after what I had done to him. He circled his fingers around me, and then pushed two of them inside of me. He drew his fingers out slowly, distributing my slick wetness around. While rubbing my clit with his thumb in an easy, circular motion, he slid his fingers back inside me.

His other hand was cupping my breast and lightly teasing my nipple. I was so aroused, I couldn't think straight. I tilted my head back as he ran his free hand up and away from my breast to cup the back of my head. He wound his fingers into my hair and held me still. His mouth again found mine, and he darted his tongue in and out quickly, teasing me.

*Oh God.*

I felt my body start to tighten and tremble from his touch, and heat seared through me as I slowly rocked my hips forward against his hand. He slid his fingers further inside of me, and the heel of his hand massaged my clit.

My orgasm hit me like a freight train. I gasped and moaned as I rested my forehead on his chest. I had to grip his arms for balance, because it felt like my knees would buckle beneath me at any time.

We stood and held onto each other until the water started to turn cool. Eventually, we rinsed off and stepped out of the shower before the water became too cold.

Covered with goose bumps, I pulled the only towel off the towel rack and wrapped it around his waist. I stood on my toes to drape my arms around his neck.

He slid his arms around me and lifted me off the floor until he was standing straight. "Good morning," I whispered in his ear.

"I don't know what's gotten in to you, Zoey, but thank you. I want to start every day like this."

Gently, he set me back on my feet, turned and pulled a towel out of the cabinet, and then wrapped it around me. He pulled another towel out, dried my arms and shoulders, and then urged me to turn around and began to towel dry my hair.

I loved how he cared for me. No man had ever treated me the way he did. I knew I was completely in love with him and would do anything to please him. Did he feel the same about me?

# Chapter Twenty-Two

When we were back in his bedroom, I had so many emotions overtake my head and heart. I felt content and loved for the first time in my life by a man. Not *loved* as in Andy was *in* love with me, because I didn't know if he felt that way about me, but I felt...treasured.

I knew he wanted to see where things went with us, but that might mean many different things. The feelings I had for him were so much more than anything I'd ever felt in my life. They weren't the same feelings I ever had with Rob. This was much more intense. These feelings were radiating from my very soul.

*Is this what a real and true love felt like with a man?* I had no idea, because apparently, I'd never been in love until now. And because no man had ever loved me, the situation was very new, and it was very overwhelming all of a sudden. I had too many thoughts swimming around in my head. Andy was searching through his dresser for clothes, so he wasn't paying attention to me for the moment.

I looked around for my pajamas and remembered I left them in the bathroom. When I went in to get them, I closed the bathroom door behind me.

As soon as my pajamas were back on, my emotions consumed me, and I needed to sit down. It had been a while since that had happened to me. I needed a minute or two to gather my composure, so I sat on the cold tile floor with my back resting against the bathtub.

I'd been sitting there for several minutes when there was a knock on the door. "You alright in there, Beautiful?" Andy asked.

"Yeah, I just needed a minute," I replied, my voice shaking.

"Can I come in please, Zoey?" he asked calmly from the other side of the door.

I could tell he knew something was off by the tone of his voice. He sounded worried, but had no reason to be. I would never do anything to hurt him again or make him doubt my feelings for him.

"It's unlocked," I called out, letting him know it was okay for him to come in.

Andy opened the door and came to sit beside me on the floor. He didn't push me, just simply sat and waited until I was ready to speak.

Patience was what I had asked him for, and it was what I was getting. He was already dressed for work in his dark blue uniform, so I knew it was getting late. *Say something, Zoey!* My conscience screamed at me.

"Andy, I swear to you I'm fine. I got a little stressed out for a minute." I tilted my head over to rest on his shoulder for comfort. As soon as I touched him, I started to relax and my mind started to calm.

"Have you ever been blindsided by something so suddenly, that you didn't know how to handle it? Something so out of your control, you just needed to sit and take it all in?"

As soon as the questions came out of my mouth, I regretted them. He'd lost his entire family in the blink of an eye.

He had been completely, tragically blindsided.

Feeling like a complete jerk, I straddled his lap, facing him, my hands resting on his chest. "Of course you have, I'm sorry. What a horrible question." I searched his eyes for the acknowledgment that he knew I was referring to his family.

It didn't take more than a second to get it. I rubbed my fingertips through the whiskers along his jawline on either side of his face. I knew he was going to do it himself, like he always did when we talked about his family. I'm not sure he even realized he did it, but I definitely noticed.

I gave him a light kiss on his nose, right on top of his scar. I knew losing his family still broke his heart, and it killed me to see the pain in his eyes.

"I've been completely blindsided three times in my life, Zoey," he said thoughtfully, after a minute. "When my parents and sister were killed, when I came home to divorce papers sitting on the table, and the last time was in this room, when you came in here this morning. What made you do it?"

"I don't know. I can't explain why I did it. I felt like I needed to please you somehow. Like I needed you to see how I feel about you. I'm sorry, is this making any sense to you?"

He looked me in the eyes. "It makes sense, and I feel the same way. I want you to know I loved every second of it." He kissed me, then held my hand flat over his heart and covered it with his. I don't think he even realized he did it because it was such an effortless movement.

It was getting late, and we needed to be at work soon, even though I would rather spend all day with him. I pressed my lips to his. "We should get to work," I grumbled between kisses.

It was daylight outside already, and there was no way I was walking back across the courtyard in my pajamas and fuzzy slippers. With my luck, I would run in to my dad or brothers coming to work early.

"Can you do me a huge favor?" I asked him.

"Anything," he mumbled as he kissed me.

"Can you go over to my apartment and get me some clothes?" I laughed and glanced down at my pj's. "I can't exactly go outside looking like this. You never know who's going to arrive at the shop to start work early."

He shot me a cocky half-smile as he peeked down at my lack of clothing. "No, I guess you can't go out like that, can you? You can always stay here all day, so I can come to see you on my breaks and lunch and have my way with you."

That had us both laughing after my shock wore off. All I could think at that very moment, was I totally would've let him. However, we needed to get to work and try to keep our relationship away from work time. It was now our rule, not only mine.

After I lifted myself from his lap, I helped him off the floor.

"What do you want me to get for you while I'm at your place?"

I thought for a minute. "I'll need everything. Jeans, shirt, socks, my Chucks, panties, bra, toothbrush, and my hairbrush. I think that should cover it."

That gorgeous, wicked grin of his spread across his face, while he, no doubt, had dirty thoughts about something. "I get to go through your panty drawer and pick out what you should wear?"

I smiled sweetly and nodded. "Yes, sir, I'll wear anything you choose."

He flipped his wrist to look at his watch. "Twenty minutes till eight, I'd better get going." Andy smiled and rubbed the palms of his hands together excitedly, then gave me a kiss on the lips. "I'll be back in a minute."

Fifteen minutes later, he came back with a bag full of my belongings.

"What took you so long?" I asked impatiently as I unpacked the bag.

"I had a really hard time picking out the panties and bra I wanted to picture you wearing all day. You have a lot of racy things in your drawer, you know? I'm kinda thinking I like that Victoria's Secret store."

*That's what I thought.* I glanced over at him, and he was grinning like a kid in a candy store. "Did you like rifling through my underwear, Andy?"

"Oh, yes. Very much, actually," he replied mischievously. "Zoey, for future reference, you should never send a horny man to pick out your underwear."

He really needed to get to work, so I attempted to send him on his way. "Get to work, Sexy. We don't want boss lady punishing you, now do we?"

He started unbuttoning his shirt with a naughty grin on his face. "Fuck that. I'm staying home, now. I could probably use a good spanking or two!"

Oh. My. God. This conversation was going to the gutter fast. But it was fun, so I decided to go with it. I walked over and swatted him hard on his very firm ass. It actually stung my hand, so I am sure it stung him a little too.

"Go to work, now!" I giggled and then rubbed my hand across where I smacked him to relieve the sting. "You're gonna be late and boss lady frowns on being tardy."

He grasped my face in his hands and kissed me hard. "See you later." With that, he turned and was out the door.

Lucky for him, he only had to go down a flight of stairs and through the back door to get to work. I was definitely going to be late. Oh well, it was worth it.

I sorted the clothing he brought me on his bed and found he did really well picking out my clothes. Of course, he chose some red, super lacy boy cut panties and a matching bra for me to wear. I assumed he liked those the best. I changed and threw my pajamas and the panties I was wearing into his clothes hamper.

My hair was crazy, and I had forgotten to ask him to bring my blow dryer, so I brushed it as flat as I could get it. Not being able to condition it at his place, it took a few extra minutes to detangle. I would end up putting it in a ponytail when I went to work anyway.

When I was finished brushing my teeth, I added my toothbrush to the toothbrush holder next to his. *Might as well leave it here, since he has one at my place.*

As I walked through the apartment to leave, I noticed he'd unpacked all of his boxes since the last time I was there. He had framed photos displayed on the living room walls and tables.

From the end table, I picked up a photo of Andy and his family. He looked like he was around fifteen years old at the time. His sister seemed quite a bit younger than he was. In the photo, they were on a beach. A huge white beach house was behind them, and the entire family was smiling and happy. Andy resembled his dad, with the same eyes and hair color.

They were a lovely family, and he was so very lucky to have had them.

Looking at the photo made me sad for him. He had lost everyone close to him. I never had anyone until I was adopted, so I didn't really know what it was like to lose someone to death. My grandmother died when I was twenty, but she'd been sick for a while, and we were expecting it.

As Andy had mentioned earlier, he had been completely blindsided when his family died. It's totally different if you know it's coming. Suddenly, I felt the urge to talk to my mom. I found Andy's phone and called her.

"Hi, Mom," I said when she answered the phone.

"Hola, Mija, how are you?" she asked. "Are you calling from Andy's?"

*Darn caller ID.* "Yeah, I am. I was visiting him. He went to work already, so I thought I would call you to say hi and see if you're doing family dinner on Sunday. I'd like to invite Andy, if you don't mind."

"Of course, I don't mind, Zoey. He's welcome here anytime, so you don't need to ask," she replied. I heard the smile in her voice, and it made me smile myself.

We talked a while longer about what we were going to fix for dinner on Sunday. After we hung up, I headed over to the store to see how the morning was going so far. It looked like it was going to be another busy day. It finally dawned on me that the store and shop were so busy due to the weather.

# Chapter Twenty-Three

Nor Cal was in a constant state of drought, and although it was chilly outside, we were not getting any rain. The store and shop business was beginning to pick up because of it. I had work to do at the shop that day, so I finished what I needed to at the store, and went to the shop. Before I sat down at my desk to go through the mail, I glanced out the window to the closest work bay, which happened to be Andy's.

I was feeling a little flirty after our shower that morning, so I sent him a text while he was working underneath a car that was high in the air on the car lift.

> *Can you stop looking so sexy in those pants? You're very distracting. Love the short sleeves too. I can see your tattoos when you lift up your arms.*

I hit send before I changed my mind.

A minute later, he fished his cell phone out of his back pocket. Andy read the message and laughed as he glanced back in the direction of the office. He dropped the grease rag he was holding in his hand onto the floor in front of him, and then slowly bent over to pick it up.

To tease me further, he reached up and did something to the undercarriage of the car, but when he did it, he flexed his biceps. He shot me a wicked grin over his shoulder as he did so. My pretending to be shocked by his actions only made him laugh even more.

Thank God the office phone rang a second later. I shouldn't be distracting him like that at work. I broke our rule. *Not good, Zoey. Not good.*

At lunchtime, he came into the office and asked me if I would like to go on our first official date with him that night. Of course, I agreed.

After work, I took a shower, picked out an outfit to wear, and did my hair and makeup. I was ready to go a little early, so I decided to turn on some music. I picked a book from my bookshelf and headed to the couch to read while I waited for Andy.

After a while, I heard a knock on my door. A second later, a key slid into the lock. The door opened, and Andy stepped inside the apartment.

He was wearing a pair of fitted jeans, faded in all the right places, and a white button-up shirt with the sleeves rolled to his elbows. The bright white of the shirt and the golden hue of his hair and skin had turned his eyes to a bright cornflower blue.

"Um, Andy...I thought we were just doing dinner and a movie, so I didn't need to dress up?"

"What do you mean?"

I smirked. Did the man not know how fucking gorgeous he was? I stood, walked over to him, and gave him a kiss. Yep, I could not keep my hands *or* lips off him. "Let me put it this way, I will probably be beating girls off with a stick to keep them away from you."

He raised his eyebrows and chuckled. He didn't seem to believe me. I took his hand in mine and dragged him to my bedroom, where I planted him in front of my full-length mirror.

"Look at you!" I exclaimed while he checked himself out in the mirror.

Jokingly, he turned and looked at his ass, and then flexed his muscles for me.

"You are absolutely, by far, the sexiest man I have ever seen in my life," I stated matter-of-factly. "Why are you here with *me*?"

An annoyed expression washed over his face. He pulled me in front of him, so I faced the mirror too. "Zoey, don't say things like that. Look at you. You are perfect. I don't ever want to hear you say something like that again, alright?"

Our eyes locked on each other in the mirror.

"Now look at *us*," he said as he stepped beside me.

Doing what he asked, I observed us together in the mirror, and I had to admit, we looked good together. Both of us were tall and lean. Whereas I was feminine, he was masculine, and each of us had different shades of blue eyes and blond hair.

"I'm sorry, you're right. I'm a little hard on myself sometimes, I guess." I studied us again in the mirror. We appeared happy and content. When was the last time I could say I was happy? I honestly couldn't remember, but I knew it was because of Andy, so I turned and kissed him. "Let's get out of here."

Andy took me to an Italian restaurant I'd never been to before, and we sat in a small booth near the front of the dining area. It was nice and cozy, with a red and white checkered tablecloth and a large candle in the center of the table. I slid into the booth, and instead of him sitting across from me, he slid right in next to me. The waiter handed us menus and took our drink orders.

Andy placed his hand on my thigh and rested it there while we scanned over our menus. I loved being so close to him. The waiter came back with our drinks, and we ordered our food.

"Are you still going to help me buy a laptop this weekend, so I can see you while you're gone on vacation?"

My heart sank a little from his reminder. I hadn't forgotten about it, but I was trying not to think about leaving for a month. I was going to miss him like crazy.

"Of course I'm going to. There's no way I'm leaving here without a way to see you while I'm gone. I'm not sure if I even want to go now," I said sullenly.

He reached over to stroke my cheek with his fingertips. "As much as I'm going to miss you, I know you need a vacation. You've been through a lot lately and deserve a nice long break, but you better promise me you won't go there and find someone else."

I looked him in the eyes. "Remember what you told me in front of the mirror earlier?" He nodded. "I don't want to hear you say that again either."

He kissed me on the cheek and then the lips. "Okay, Beautiful."

As soon as our food arrived, we ate as quickly as possible to make the late show. Fortunately, the theater was close to the restaurant, and we made it to our seats right as the movie started. Not that we saw much of the movie. Turns out it was terrible, and we were more interested in each other. We left the theater early and went back to his place.

"Sorry about the movie," he said as we sat down on his couch.

"I don't mind. It's been a long week, so I was a little tired anyway," I admitted. I remembered about family dinner on Sunday. "Oh, by the way, you're invited to family dinner on Sunday. You game?"

He smiled. "Of course I'll come. Should I bring anything?"

"Nope, Mom and I are going to barbecue some steaks. You can play cards with the guys while we're cooking."

"Sounds good to me," he replied.

I leaned back onto the throw pillow and stretched, covering a yawn with my hand.

"Are you going to stay here with me tonight?" he asked.

"Do you want me to?" *I hope so.*

He stood and held his hand out to me. "Of course I do. Let's go to bed." *Yes, please.* He hoisted me off the couch and shut off the lights, and we walked to his bedroom.

He pulled two drawers open on his dresser, grabbed a pair of flannel shorts out for himself, and handed me a T-shirt. I went into the bathroom to get ready for bed. I brushed my teeth, stripped down to my panties, and pulled the plain black shirt over my head. It was super soft, like the New Zealand shirt I stole from him. It also barely covered my butt.

After I finished in the bathroom, I went back to his bedroom.

"I'll be right back. Hurry and get in bed. It's cold in here."

On his way to the bathroom, he turned up the thermostat on the control panel in the hallway. It was freezing, so I huddled under the covers to try to rid myself of my goose bumps. When he was ready for bed, he climbed in next to me.

"Zoey, your legs are so cold," he said as his bare legs brushed against mine. "Let me get you some of my flannel pants." He started to get out of bed to get them.

"No," I said, shivering from the cold. "Stay. I'll be warmer now that you're in here."

Andy let out a long sigh. "Fine, be that way," he said, sarcastically.

He stripped off his flannel shorts, pulled them out from under the covers, and threw them over his tattooed shoulder onto the floor. "You'll get warm faster this way, at least." He smiled his most smoldering smile. "I hope you can handle my bedroom attire for one night," he said, draping his arm over me and scooting closer.

I laughed. "I think we threw that rule out the window this morning, don't you?" He could wear what he wanted to bed. On the other hand, he could wear nothing at all. I was fine with it, now that I'd seen him completely naked and had my hands and mouth all over him. I also knew I would have a hard time resisting him, no matter what he was wearing.

But, I promised myself not to move any faster than we already had. I frowned when my mind drifted away from my happy thoughts. This was a big step for me, and I was still overwhelmed with my feelings for him. Feelings that were completely new to me.

"What were you thinking just now?" he asked. "You got the exact same look on your face this morning. Is everything alright?"

"Yeah, sorry, I'm fine," I lied.

He caressed my face and combed my hair back over my ear. "Zoey, don't lie to me. If this is moving too fast for you, we can slow down. I don't want to lose you by going too fast. After this morning, it will be hard but—"

"Andy?" I interrupted. He was lying so close to me, I could feel his erection pressed against my belly.

"Yeah?" he replied seriously.

"It feels like it's already *hard*," I joked, giggling as I ran my hand over the front of his boxer briefs and gave him a firm squeeze.

He sucked in a shocked breath. "God, I love you, Zoey," he groaned, as he flipped me onto my back.

We laughed as we wrestled around playfully, and he pushed my legs apart. Andy hovered over me, pressing his erection directly where I desperately wanted it to be. I would rather it was without the two thin pieces of fabric from our underwear in the way though.

*Fuck.* He stared me right in the eyes and rocked his hips forward, pressing harder against me. I wanted him so badly right then, but I knew better.

"I'm not ready for sex yet, but everything else is fair game," I told him as I pushed his boxers down over his ass and hips.

Still hovering over me, he moved in to kiss me. "Whatever you want is fine with me," he mumbled with his lips pressed against mine.

Once he was completely naked, I wound my fingers around his rigid cock and started stroking him. He broke our kiss, and then sat up on his knees in between mine, causing me to lose my grip on him.

He helped me to a sitting position and pulled his shirt off over my head, leaving me wearing only my panties. I laid back and dragged him down with me, which caused his bare erection to press firmly against me.

We returned to kissing each other, our tongues entwined. He pushed the head of his cock against me harder, repeatedly. God, I wanted him inside me. I wrapped my fingers around him again and began stroking as he pushed slightly into me through my soaked panties. I wasn't sure I could stop at that point. All my will was about to leave me.

I released him, wrapped my arms around him, and lightly raked my fingernails up his back to his shoulders while I ground myself against him. Andy tilted his hips and the head of his cock pressed hard against my clit. I gasped, feeling my body ache for him. He did it again, and again. The last time did me in, and my orgasm took over.

"*Ahh, Andy,*" I moaned as I wound my fingers once again around him, resting his heavy cock between my palm and my bare belly.

He thrust his hips forward and back, as if he were inside of me, his cock nestled tightly between my hand and my stomach. I was starting to feel a little friction between our bodies, when he abruptly reached down between my legs and inside my panties. He slid two fingers inside of me, briefly sliding them in and out.

When his fingers and hand were slippery from the wetness of my orgasm, he took his cock into his own hand, and began stroking it to coat himself with my slick fluids.

*Holy. Fucking. Hell.*

Okay, now *that* was officially the most erotic thing I'd ever seen in my life.

I took over stroking him again, and within minutes, he was moaning my name and collapsing on top of me, his warm wetness covering my belly. I nipped his ear lightly with my teeth, and his body trembled against mine again.

"Jesus, Zoey," he groaned after a minute. "What are you doing to me?"

"The same thing you're doing to me," I whispered.

We laid there in complete silence before Andy rolled off the bed and went to the bathroom. I heard the water running in the sink, and then him opening and closing the cabinet door.

He came back into the bedroom with a wet, hand towel. I reached out for it, so I could clean myself off. "I'll do it," he said as he straddled me, still completely naked. He took the towel and very gently wiped off my stomach. I started to pull the covers back up over me after he finished.

"I'm not done with you," he said huskily as he threw the towel onto the floor and pulled the blankets completely off me.

*Oh my.*

# Chapter Twenty-Four

Andy said nothing as he sat back on his heels on the floor beside the bed. He hooked his fingers under the waistband of my panties and slowly pulled them off me. Staring at me hungrily, he ran his tongue over his lips to moisten them.

"I wish you could see how fucking beautiful you look right now, Zoey," he said, his deep voice laced with desire.

He tossed my panties aside, and then carefully pulled me to the edge of the bed by my ankles. Slowly, he pushed my knees apart as a sexy grin eased over his face. *Oh fuck, is this really happening?* My eyes would not close. I wanted to watch him while he devoured me.

Kneeling on the floor at the edge of the bed, he lifted my foot, placing it on his tattooed shoulder. Starting at my ankle, he slowly licked and kissed his way up my leg. *Oh, sweet Jesus.* He worked his way to the inside of my thigh so slowly I felt I would die from anticipation.

This was one thing I'd *never* had done to me, and with the way Andy was looking at me, I knew I was going to enjoy every second of it.

One of his hands slid up my body, delicately squeezing my breast and teasing my nipple. With his other hand, he slid his fingers inside me. After another agonizing minute, I finally felt his mouth on me. He kissed and licked my clit at first, and then he slowly removed his fingers and replaced them with his warm, wet tongue. *Holy fucking hell.*

He moaned softly as he licked, sucked, and teased me, repeatedly flicking his tongue hard over my clit. He then sucked it in between his lips while he moaned louder. The vibration from that, and the slight tickle from his stubble touching other sensitive parts of me, sent me careening over the edge. My orgasm seemed to go on forever, because once it began, he did not let up on me.

When I finally stopped shuddering, he gave one last lick and then ran his tongue back to my clit, which he kissed softly before pulling away from me. My thumping heart and breathing eventually slowed, but I was so spent, I literally could not move.

"Wow," was all I could say after the most amazing sexual experience of my life, to date.

After one last kiss on the inside of my thigh, he picked me up to lie beside him. Andy turned off the lamp and pulled the covers over us.

"Goodnight, Beautiful," he whispered.

Even though I was tired and completely sated, I could not fall asleep because my mind kept straying to something he had said.

He said he loved me.

How was I supposed to take it? What if I said it back, and the way I wanted him to mean it, wasn't the way he meant it? We were joking around right before he said the words, so I truly wasn't sure. I decided to keep quiet and eventually drifted off to sleep.

The next thing I knew, it was morning, and I slept in until nine-thirty. I hadn't slept so soundly, or so long, in ages. I rolled over and found Andy propped up on his elbow, watching me.

"Good morning," I whispered sleepily as I snuggled myself into the crook of his neck and chest, draping my arm over his side. Why was he always so warm and comforting?

Slowly, I opened my eyes and moved my hand down his body. He was naked, freshly showered, and absolute perfection. I explored his tattoos with my fingertips, tracing the tribal outlines over his chest. "What does this one represent?"

He didn't even look down to see which tattoo I was referring to. "If you look closely, it's the New Zealand islands. The swirling designs around them represent the Pacific Ocean and the Tasman Sea."

He had New Zealand tattooed right over his heart. It made me sad because I knew he missed his home country.

"I've always wanted to get one. How bad does it hurt?" I nestled back in to the crook of his neck and shoulder, and closed my eyes.

"It depends," he started, "on what you want to get, and where you want it on your body. What kind of tattoo do you want to get?"

I started to drift back to sleep. "Snowflakes," I murmured.

"Why does that not surprise me?" he replied, laughing quietly.

Sometime later, I awoke to him massaging my bare back. "Wake up, sleepy head. It's getting late, and you promised to go shopping with me today, remember? Come on. Let's get you in the shower."

I rolled out of bed completely naked and pushed my crazy hair away from my face. "Okay, okay. I'm up," I groaned as I strolled across the hallway to the bathroom with my eyes half-open. He whistled at me as I went into the bathroom. *God, he makes me happy,* I thought as I grabbed a towel from the towel closet.

I took a nice hot shower by myself. Reaching out to pick up his body soap, I found my body soap was next to his. My shampoo and conditioner were there too. He'd gone over to my place, while I was asleep, and gathered all my shower products for me to use, so I didn't have to use his or go home.

After I finished in the shower, I entered his bedroom with a towel wrapped around me. On his bed, he had laid out several pieces of clothing from my closet. He brought two of everything: shirts, jeans, bras, panties. *Everything.* He even brought my blow dryer.

"Are you hungry?" he asked from the doorway.

I turned to face him and he was dressed in old faded jeans and a dark blue T-shirt. He was barefoot and breathtaking, as usual.

A feeling of complete inadequacy washed over me. What was this man doing with me? No doubt, he could have any girl he wanted, but here I was, in his bedroom, with him catering to me. I began feeling a bit overwhelmed again.

"You went and got all this for me?" I asked. He nodded, appearing to be confused as to what the issue was. "Thank you...but why me?" Nobody had ever done anything like that for me. It was such a simple gesture, but it really meant a great deal. Nobody except the James family ever put me first. *Not even me.*

"I think you know why, Zoey," he said quietly as he stepped closer to me. "Are you going to pretend you didn't hear what I told you last night?"

No, I heard him, loud and clear. *"God, I love you, Zoey."*

"I heard what you said," I admitted. "I wasn't sure how I was supposed to interpret it. You said it while you were laughing, and we were playing around. I didn't know if you said it because you loved what I said before you told me, or if you really meant..." *That you love me. Me.*

He stood in front of me, but didn't touch me. "If I told you it was both, would it make sense?"

I shrugged my shoulders, not knowing what to say. I needed to sit down and collapsed onto the edge of his bed. He dropped to his knees at my feet and my heart skipped a beat at the sight of the gorgeous man kneeling in front of me.

"I'm sorry, Zoey. It just came out, because it was what I was feeling at the time. Do you have any idea what you do to me? It's not easy for me to feel the way I do about you, knowing you're probably going to push me away."

He was annoyed, so I reached out and pulled him closer to me. I had previously made a promise to myself that I would never hurt him again, and I intended to keep that promise. I needed to put myself out there, lay it on the line, so to speak.

I pressed my forehead to his and rested my palms along his jawline. "Do you think this is easy for me?" Now I was the one getting upset, but not at him. I was angry for being so scared and stupid and for doubting myself.

"I've never had these feelings for anyone. I told you yesterday I was feeling a little stressed. When I get this way, I panic and shut down, but I swear I won't push you away again. I'm in this with you, don't you get that?"

My eyes filled with tears. "Do you know how fucking tired I am of being this way? Sometimes I need a minute to get the thoughts right in my head."

I was pretty much in full meltdown mode at that point and unable to stop it.

"For over half of my life, I was thrown away by people who were supposed to love me and take care of me. Now, here you are, willing to give me everything I've ever wanted, and I am scared that somehow I'll screw up, and then you'll leave me because of all my emotional bullshit."

He pulled his head back so we were eye to eye. "Just let me love you, Zoey. You don't have to say you love me back. I'll be patient like you asked. I won't push."

I wiped off my face with the towel that was still wrapped around me.

There he goes using my love for song lyrics again to make me see things clearly. He even picked the song we danced to on my birthday. The same song that had made him walk away from me. The same song that had made me realize I was falling in love with him.

I knew the feelings I had for him, and the feelings he had for me, had to be love. It flowed through my entire body, into my heart and soul. I guess it could happen so soon, and it definitely felt right. Even though we'd only known each other a very short time, we *knew* each other in the deepest sense of the word.

"Zoey, please say something."

I took a deep, trembling breath, and exhaled. I met his gaze. "Don't forget, you're the reason I'm here."

He brought my hand up to his face, kissed my palm, and then rested it on his cheek.

It was time for me to tell him...I needed to give in to what my heart wanted. I was conceding. I was throwing myself out there into oblivion, where I knew he would catch me. I no longer had a choice in the matters of my heart and mind.

He needed to know I loved him back.

"I love you, Andy."

Once the words were out, I let my mind and emotions go. It felt like something inside me broke. I felt defeated, yet relieved in the fact that I'd actually said the words at all. I really had nowhere to go from there but up.

He held my face in his hands, rubbing his thumbs lightly across my cheeks. Andy didn't speak. He just stared into my eyes with a look of complete love and happiness on his face.

"I said I love you."

"I heard you, Beautiful. I'm letting it sink in a minute." He finally smiled.

"I love you, too...so much," he whispered after another moment. I wound my arms around his neck and pressed my forehead to his as I took in several deep breaths.

"Andy, we know how we feel about each other, so can we chill out now?" I let go of him as he pulled back to look me in the eyes.

"Chill out, as in relax?" he asked. I nodded. "Yeah, love. We can. On one condition, though."

I raised my eyebrows, waiting for what he had to say.

"Will you please tell me as soon as you start feeling like that again? I can't stand to see you upset or sad."

"Yes. I promise." I embraced him tightly and whispered, "Let's go get you that laptop."

We finished getting ready and headed out to the electronics store. Andy drove my car, and when he pulled out onto the main road, he headed straight to Dutch Bros. and bought us coffees. He also insisted on getting me one of their delicious orange-cranberry muffin tops to eat, since I had slept through breakfast.

While he was picking out his laptop, I came up with an idea, so I told him I needed to use the bathroom. I found what I wanted, and as quickly as possible, I bought him the same iPod as mine and ran it back out to my car to hide it in the trunk.

When I finally made it back inside the store, he was finished with the salesperson.

"What happened, Beautiful? Did you fall in?" he joked, referring to the toilet.

"Ha, ha. Very funny, smartass. I got sidetracked on the way back to find you."

We looked through the movies, and he bought several DVDs to watch at my place, since he couldn't decide which television he wanted to buy. He let me buy him lunch before we went home.

# Chapter Twenty-Five

A couple of nights before at dance class, I had made plans with Jess and Sasha to go to dinner and see a movie for that night. It would be the first evening Andy and I had spent apart since we started our relationship.

"Did you find something to do for the night?" I asked Andy after we set up his laptop and linked it to the shop's Wi-Fi.

"Jeremy asked if I wanted to go to the bar with him and his friends. I might go and have a beer or two with them."

*Great.* My single brother, Jeremy, AKA "the Chick Magnet." He and his friends would be swarmed with girls at the bar all night long. I knew I had no reason to be jealous, especially after our discussion earlier that day.

"Well, have fun, but watch out for Jeremy's groupies."

He pulled me close and kissed me. "Don't worry. I love *you*, remember?"

How could I forget? I kissed him back. "I'll see you tomorrow morning. Enjoy your night out and be careful, please."

He kissed me goodnight. "You too."

I headed across the courtyard, making a quick stop at my car to grab the bag containing the iPod I bought for him. I went upstairs to my place and got ready for my date with Jess and Sasha.

We had a great night, ate good food, saw a new chick flick, and afterwards we went out for coffee and dessert. It was like old times, and I was so thankful and happy my two best friends forgave me for pushing them away.

Once I arrived at home, I noticed Andy's truck was in the parking lot. It was barely after eleven, so it surprised me that he was home so early. All the lights were off at his place, so I went home. I didn't want to wake him if he was asleep, and we had already agreed to see each other the next morning.

I stepped inside my apartment and found his shoes sitting beside the door. He was at my place, not his. My bedroom light was on, so I strolled down the hallway, excited to see him. Andy was sitting up in my bed, reading a car magazine.

"Hey," he said as I walked through the doorway. "How was the movie?"

I loved the fact that he was in my bed waiting for me to get home. I stripped down to my panties, plucked his T-shirt out of my top drawer, and pulled it over my head.

"We had a lot of fun. The movie was good, and dinner was great too. How'd your night go?" I asked.

He actually groaned, and not in a good way. *Uh oh.* I would need to fix his bad groan to a good groan later.

"What happened?" I asked.

Andy took a deep breath and let it out. "First, let me say thanks for the warning about Jeremy's groupies," he laughed. "We got to the bar and had a few beers...played darts and pool. That girl, Nicole, was there and she would not back off."

*Ugh, I'm not sure if I want to hear any more.* I really didn't like calling people names or anything, but Nicole really was a skank. She never took no for an answer. In fact, if someone told her no, it made her work harder for what she wanted.

In the last few years, she had systematically gone through my brother and all of his friends. Twice.

Jeremy had a lot of friends.

"Andy, did you...?" my question trailed off.

He sat straight up so abruptly it caught me off guard. "Hell no, Zoey! You really don't think I'd do that, do you?"

I sat up with him, feeling terrible I even asked him, when I knew deep down, he wouldn't.

"Of course not, but I know how *she* is. What happened?"

He sat for a minute, not saying anything. I felt like I needed to lighten the mood a bit, so I crawled over to him on the bed and sat on his lap, facing him.

"Sexy, do you want me to go find her and beat her up?" I joked. "Because I totally will, if you want me to."

He chuckled. "No, Zoey, I think I took care of it."

I felt a bit of relief. "Did *you* beat her up?"

"No, smartass, I did not beat her up."

I loved the easy banter back and forth with him. "So, tell me what happened," I said, looking into his beautiful blue eyes.

"We'd been at the bar for a while when she and a few of her friends showed up. They joined us, and she started talking to me because she remembered me from the party next door. She was drunk and came right out and actually asked me if I wanted to go to the bathroom and fuck her."

*That fucking little bitch.* My mouth dropped open slightly, and he looked disgusted. "Go on," I said through clenched teeth.

"Of course, I told her no, that I have a girlfriend, and I wasn't interested. She said something like, 'your loss' and walked off. About twenty minutes later, I'm standing at the bar with Jeremy's friend, John, waiting for a beer, and she comes up behind me, reaches around and grabs my—"

I didn't let him finish what he was saying, because I started laughing hysterically.

An expression of amused confusion washed over his face. "You're not mad at me?"

"Why would I be mad at you? Of course, I'm mad, because she grabbed my man's junk, but I told you before that I know how she is. What you're saying is no surprise to me. She has gone through my brother and his friends at least twice that I know of. You are fresh meat to her. Besides, look at you. You're gorgeous, and that accent of yours is hot as hell."

I laughed again at the shocked expression on his face. "Looks like I've got some competition."

He shook his head and smiled. "No way, Zoey; there is no competition. All I want is you, not some man-crazy chick who goes around grabbing your 'man's junk,' as you so fondly called my dick," he laughed.

Where did this man come from? Most men would've taken her to the bathroom like she wanted and never thought twice about it. In fact, I know several have.

Jokingly, I cupped my hand around my ear, pretending I hadn't heard him. "I'm sorry, Sexy. You want your junk fondled, is that what you said?"

He began laughing so hard his eyes started watering. "As long as it's you doing the fondling, then the answer is yes!"

He stopped laughing and became serious.

"Zoey, Jeremy saw what happened." *Shit.* "He asked me if I was trying to hook up with her. I told him no, but he was still mad."

*Oh, fuck.*

"What happened next?" I asked.

He took a breath. "I tried to explain to him what she did, but I'm not sure if he believed me or not. He was pretty shit-faced."

*Sounds like Jeremy.*

"Are you sure I'm worth all this crap you have to put up with?" I asked him, only half-joking.

"I know you are. You mean everything to me." He gently cupped my face in his hands and kissed me, pulling me over on top of him when he leaned back against the pillows.

After a nice long make-out session, I rolled off him and pulled my cell from my purse to call Jeremy. I didn't give a damn what time it was or what he might be in the middle of doing.

He answered after the fifth ring, "Huhllooo," he slurred, obviously still out drinking with his friends.

"Jeremy, it's Zoey. You need to sober the fuck up for a few minutes, so I can have a word with you."

"Zoey!" he yelled into the phone, and a second later, I heard his friends echo "Zoey!" in the background. They sure liked to go out and have a good time, like a bunch of fucking jackasses.

"Jeremy, I need to talk about what happened with Andy at the bar." Silence. "Jeremy? I wanted to let you know Andy and I talked about what happened at the bar with Nicole. You had no reason to be a dick to him. He's a good guy."

Silence.

"Jer, did you hear me?" I asked, wondering if he'd fallen asleep or passed out.

"Yeah, Z, I heard you. John was with him and told me the same thing Andy did. I feel like an ass now. I was only trying to protect you after the issues with that douchebag, Rob. I don't want to see you get hurt again. I'm sorry. Please forgive me?"

"Sure thing, dumb-fuck. All is forgiven. Just don't let it happen again."

He let out chuckle. "Thanks, Z. By the way, I've never seen Nicole so pissed that he turned her down. She actually left with Rob when he showed up after Andy left."

*Wonderful.* "Goodnight, Jer. See you tomorrow at dinner."

"Well?" Andy asked after my call ended.

"It's all good. With as much as he's been drinking, he will probably forget all about it by tomorrow. I'm sorry he did that though. He's a little protective of me."

I tossed my phone back inside my purse. I was exhausted, so I slid down into the bed. Andy turned off his lamp and laid down with me, pulling the covers over us.

"Get some sleep. I'll make you a nice breakfast in the morning," I told him.

"I love you, Zoey," he whispered.

I could really get used to hearing that. I gave him a long, tender kiss, "I love you, too," I replied and closed my eyes.

A minute later, I heard Andy chuckling quietly.

"What's so funny over there?"

He slid closer to me. "Can you fondle my junk now, please?"

After we stopped laughing, we fondled each other until we fell asleep.

Surprisingly, the next morning, I woke before Andy, and I was craving French toast. I showered and dressed, and then went into the kitchen to start breakfast. I was whisking the eggs when I heard the shower turn on in my bedroom.

I wanted to repay Andy somehow for what he did the previous day, when he had gone to my apartment and gathered all the things I needed to get ready for the day. I was certain he didn't want to smell like a girl from using my shampoo and soap.

I took his keys and jogged across the courtyard to his apartment. I went in and found everything he would need, and then started back over to my place.

When I stepped off the bottom stair, I heard a high-pitched cry of some sort. Unsure if I was hearing things, I stopped and listened. Then I heard it again. It was coming from over by Andy's car trailer.

As soon as I got closer to the trailer, I saw a tiny orange colored fluff ball huddled behind the tire. *A kitten!* I knelt down and picked it up. It was still crying and shivering from being so cold.

"Where did you come from, little baby?"

It was so tiny. I looked around for a mama cat, but didn't find one. I pulled off my hoody, wrapped the kitty in it to warm it up, and took it back to my apartment.

Andy was still in the shower, so I went into the bathroom. "Hey, look what I found," I called out.

He pulled the shower curtain back and stuck his head out to see. "Is that a cat?" he asked, his face wet and soapy.

"Yes, it was under your car trailer. I went to get your soap and shampoo for your shower and heard it crying."

He held his hand out, so I handed his soap and shampoo to him. "Finish up in there and come help me. I don't know what to do with it."

I went to the laundry room and put the kitten, still wrapped in my hoody, into an empty laundry basket and took it to the kitchen with me. It crawled around the basket crying for a few minutes, and then curled up and went to sleep.

I washed my hands and went back to making breakfast. Andy came into the kitchen dressed in jeans and a T-shirt. He was barefoot, as usual.

"Can you possibly get any sexier?" I asked him, giving him a once over.

"I could ask the same of you," he replied. Coming over to where I was at the stove, he wrapped his arms around my waist. Resting his stubbly chin on my shoulder, he watched as I soaked a slice of bread in egg wash and dropped it in the pan with some melted butter.

"That smells good," he said. "You smell good, too. Where'd your new little friend go?"

"Over in the laundry basket," I motioned toward the dining room entrance.

He sat down on the floor next to the basket, picked up the kitten, then wrapped it safely back in my hoody. "What are you going to do with it?" He began scratching the sleeping kitten behind its ears.

Good question. I had thought about getting a cat, but decided against it because I pictured myself as a crazy spinster cat lady. I had a man in my life now, so that wasn't going to happen. However, if he did leave me, I would already have a cat to begin my spinsterhood.

Either way, it sounded like a win-win situation for the kitten. "I guess I should keep it." *Just in case...*

"We'll need to get it some food soon, Zoey. It's probably starving."

I slid the French toast onto two plates, drizzled them with melted butter, and dusted them with powdered sugar. "Eat your breakfast, and then we'll run to the pet store when we're done."

He carefully laid the kitten back in the basket and washed his hands to eat breakfast. I fixed his coffee the way he liked it, and then poured a cup for myself, adding Hazelnut creamer and sugar. As I stirred my coffee, he dug into his French toast with enthusiasm.

"Jesus, Zoey. This is good. I've never had it fixed this way before. It's always drowning in syrup. I like it this way better."

I smiled over at him. "Thank you. It's so bad, I put a ton of melted butter on it, then lots of powdered sugar, then squish the powdered sugar down into the butter until it turns in to a yellow, sugary, buttery paste on top of the toast. Then I'll eat it."

He took the last piece of his French toast and did just that. He popped a bite into his mouth and chewed for a few seconds, then closed his eyes, savoring the taste. "Mmm, you're right. It's so much better this way."

While I was eating my breakfast, and Andy was making himself more French toast, we talked and decided to keep the kitten.

We headed over to the pet store with the little ball of orange fur to buy it some food and anything else it would need. Between Andy and me, neither of us had owned a pet before. We knew nothing about cats, other than to feed them.

The manager at the pet store guessed the kitten was around eight weeks old and could eat solid food with no issues. He also told us it was a boy and needed a flea bath. We bought everything we would need for our new kitten and went home.

*Home.* That had a nice ring to it. We took him home and fed him, then ran warm water in the sink to bathe and rid him of the fleas.

"Poor little baby," I said sadly. "What if I hadn't found him?"

I wrapped him in a towel to warm and dry his skinny, water-soaked body. I rubbed his fur with the towel to dry him off, and he started purring loudly and seemed to fall asleep.

"He sounds like a tiny car motor," I said quietly, so I didn't wake him.

Andy chuckled and agreed. "What should we name him?" he asked.

We each tossed out a bunch of names, but nothing seemed to fit. I thought he needed a human name, and not some lame pet name like Whiskers or Sassy.

I remembered Andy's middle initial was J. "What's your middle name, Andy?" I asked, trying to think of boy names because my mind was drawing a complete blank.

His face brightened with an idea. "That's perfect, Zoey. It's James. We'll call him James," he said and then started laughing.

Too funny, my last name and his middle name were the same.

"James it is!" We gave each other a high-five.

We got James settled in his new temporary home in the laundry room. As soon as he was old enough, I would give him full run of the apartment, of course, but he would need a bit of training first. I already knew he was going to be spoiled. He had a new bed, toys, treats, and two people who cared about him.

"I feel like we adopted a kid," I laughed and turned to Andy. "Wait, that didn't sound the way it was supposed to. What I mean is, this poor little baby was abandoned, and we took him in and gave him a home. We even named him James. It kinda reminds me of...*me*. I was abandoned, and the James family took me in."

Andy watched me intently as I rambled. "Okay, I'm gonna shut up now," I said as I closed the door to the laundry room.

"I know what you meant, Zoey."

Of course he did. He *got* me.

# Chapter Twenty-Six

Over the next week, Andy and I continued our daily routines. We both worked, I went to therapy and class. We ate dinner together nightly and slept at either his place or mine.

Aside from the time we had to spend apart because of class and work, we were inseparable. It was perfect. What made it even better was we hadn't heard a peep out of Rob.

The police finally called me back, saying they found no evidence to charge him with throwing the brick through the door of my store. I was fine with it honestly, because I didn't want to deal with him ever again.

For the first time in years, I was happy, and it was because of Andy. The addition of our kitten, James, also gave us a welcome distraction.

Andy and I still hadn't had sex. We did many other things, but it was getting harder to stop ourselves.

It's not that I didn't want to make love with him, because I sure as hell did...but I still needed to wait a bit longer. We had already moved so fast in our relationship, I just didn't want to rush that part. I wanted to take pleasure in everything with him, take our time.

Thank God he agreed with me. It made it easier to endure. *For now.*

We spent our evenings, when I wasn't at dance class, watching movies and playing with James. Most of the time, when we were trying to watch a movie, we spent our time exploring each other's bodies instead. I knew he would be a generous lover, as I would be to him.

I decided to make love to him before I went to Mexico. I would be gone a month, and I didn't want to go a whole month without touching him, but I didn't have a choice. I wanted to make it special for us, but I had less than two weeks until my vacation.

I woke the day of my dance class, and the first thing I noticed was Andy. He was gone. Again. Even though I frequently woke without him in bed, I always heard him somewhere in the apartment.

This day felt different, and a sinking feeling rose in the pit of my stomach. I knew it was my own insecurities playing with my mind, but I still became a little panicked. A lifetime of people leaving me, and sending me away to new foster homes when they grew tired of me, messed with my head. I slipped out of bed and searched for him.

He was definitely not there and hadn't left a note. I looked out the window, and his truck was gone too. I brushed my teeth and washed my face, trying to keep busy, when all I wanted to do was get back in bed and pull the covers over my head.

As I walked back to my bed, I picked up my iPod from the nightstand and put in my ear buds. It was going to be one of those days. I laid there for a while, wondering if I'd done something wrong. I hated feeling like that, but it was inevitable some days. Fortunately, I had therapy later that day, and it would help to talk to Dr. Jensen.

My favorite song came on, and I let the tears roll freely from my eyes.

What if I really screwed things up? What if he was tired of my insecurities? I would never forgive myself if I lost him because of my lame shit. I took in a deep, unsteady breath and let it out, then wiped the tears off my cheek. Maybe I just needed a good cry. I had days like that. What woman didn't? I closed my eyes and listened to my music.

A few songs later, I felt something touch my hair. When I opened my eyes, Andy was kneeling at the side of my bed, trying to wake me up. I pulled out my ear buds. "I thought you left," I whispered.

"I did, but only to go get us coffee." He set two large Dutch Bros. cups on my nightstand. "Wait, what do you mean, you thought I left? As in never coming back, *left*?"

I nodded.

He pulled the covers off me and crawled, fully clothed, into bed beside me. "I'm afraid you're stuck with me now. I said I loved you, Zoey. Please never doubt that."

I leaned forward and kissed him, needing to feel our connection with each other. Our kiss quickly turned into more. I let my hands wander over his broad chest, up his neck, and into his hair. He kept his hair short, so there wasn't much for me to run my fingers through.

They didn't stay there long anyway. There were far better parts of my man's body to touch than his hair. My hands began roaming elsewhere, and mine weren't the only hands roaming.

I was still wearing my pajamas, which consisted of a tank top and boxers. He trailed his hand up my leg, where it rested under my shorts. I broke our kiss and gently bit his bottom lip, and then ran my tongue across where I had bitten.

Andy removed his hand from under my shorts and slid it under my tank top to cup my bare breast, rubbing his thumb over my nipple. I let out a quiet hum in response to his touch. I kissed him again, and then trailed kisses down his neck.

He was definitely aroused too. He was hard and hot, pressing against me. Suddenly, I didn't want to wait anymore.

While we kissed, I moved my hand down his stomach and undid the button and zipper on his jeans. As I slipped my hand inside his boxers and wrapped my fingers around him, he broke our kiss.

"Zoey, *wait*," he growled, clearly regretting his decision to stop. "As much as I really want to do this right now, we can't. I need to be to work soon, and boss lady might fire me if I am late."

*Shit, he was right.* Well, not about the firing part, but he did have to be at work soon. "Glad one of us was thinking," I sighed. "Just so you know, boss lady really isn't your boss. Her dad is. I work there just the same as you do."

He grinned deviously. "I know, but I like calling you boss lady. Makes me feel kinda naughty when I do it."

Of course, I had to laugh. "You like me bossing you around, Andy? Do you want me to keep you under control too?"

I started giggling and trying to tickle him in the ribs. He swatted at my hands, and then pinned me down with my hands over my head. He finally let go of my hands and rolled to his back after he kissed me long and hard.

He wrapped his arm over me and pulled me on top of him, resting his big hands on my hips. He was still hard, and my body was pressed exquisitely against him in all the right places. I kissed him again, and as I did, I rocked my hips forward slightly, rubbing myself against his erection. He squeezed my hips to stop me.

"Fuck, you're killing me, Zoey."

"Sorry, Sexy," I whispered in his ear before I licked the side of his neck and nipped his earlobe with my teeth. I ground my hips onto him again. *I was sooo not sorry for that!*

"You are so bad," he grumbled. "I'm gonna be walking around with a hard-on all day now."

I decided to quit torturing him, so I carefully lifted myself up, trying not to brush myself against him again. He rolled off the bed to stand and had to adjust himself before he could zip and button his pants. The vision of him standing over me on my bed, doing that, just about did me in. My resolve was definitely weak.

"Your coffee's cold now," he said with a smirk as he pulled me off the bed. "Come on, get dressed for work. I'll go home, so your brothers don't see me coming from over here and beat my ass."

He was still uncomfortable with them knowing he was sleeping at my place for some reason. He gave me a quick kiss on the lips, while I wrapped my arms around his waist to give his ass a squeeze. Instead of admonishing me for teasing him again, he returned the affection by giving mine a squeeze too.

*Yep, this is gonna be a really long day.*

That night, I headed to my dance class with Sasha and Jess. We had started a new routine the week before, so we were able to play around with it that night. Class got over a little bit late, and we walked outside to leave.

Of course, being women, we started talking when we stopped at the curb where our cars sat parked. It was dark outside, and some of the other women from the class joined in our conversation. Sirens were blaring in the distance, and I silently hoped they were not coming our way, because I was ready to go home and take a hot shower.

"Zoey, what are your plans for the weekend?" Jess asked.

"I don't really have any plans, other than dinner on Sunday with the family. What ab—"

I was cut off by Jess screaming, "Zoey, look out!" She reached out and jerked me sideways, but something huge hit me from behind and then it felt like I was flying through the air. The last thing I saw were the four circles of the Audi emblem on my own car. *Weird...*

I felt the impact, and everything went black.

I don't know how long I was unconscious, but when I opened my eyes, I saw Jess and Sasha hovering over me. My car was directly in front of me, and I was laying on my side in the street. I attempted to roll onto my back but couldn't.

"Zoey, don't move. The ambulance is on its way," Sasha cried out as tears dripped down her face.

*Ambulance? What the fuck happened?*

My eyes fluttered closed involuntarily, and I was in the dark again.

I heard sirens, and when my eyes would cooperate and open for me, I saw flashing red lights and my best friends crying while talking on their cell phones.

*This is bad.* I wanted to scream, to know what happened. *Why am I in so much pain?* My head felt like it was going to explode, my ribs hurt when I breathed, and my hip was killing me. I tasted blood in my mouth, so I ran my tongue over my teeth, praying they were all still where they were supposed to be.

*Oh God, why does my head hurt so badly?*

The black enveloped me again.

To be continued...

The second part of Zoey and Andy's story will continue in the upcoming book

**"Just Say Yes"**

# Author Bio

Jen Andrews was raised in a small town in Northern California, and still lives in the same county where she was born. She is a self-proclaimed music and lyric addict. She grew up in a 'car family' so her life has been spent around old hot rods. She and her husband, Jake, even have a few of their own. In her spare time, Jen loves to travel wherever she can. She finally lived her dream of traveling to New Zealand to see her favorite rugby team, the All Blacks, play. Jen loves to do photography as a hobby and continues to write.

Find Jen here:

https://www.goodreads.com/author/show/7762025.Jen_Andrews

https://www.facebook.com/AuthorJenAndrews